Praise for R
and his h

"Draws his memorab
bigger-than-life strokes."

—Terry C. Johnston, award-winning author of *The Plainsmen*

"Nobody does it better than Dick Wheeler . . . an extraordinary writer." —*The Roundup Quarterly*

"A taut drama about one of the most controversial issues in the modern West. [Wheeler] again demonstrates his story-telling genius in creating magnificent, believable characters. This is a fine novel and deserves a large readership. It is as timely as tomorrow's newspaper and once started, it is hard to put down. Wheeler has another award winner on his hands."—*Tulsa World*

"Wheeler has produced fiction, but the story deals with some very real issues. . . . By dramatizing and personalizing them, he makes them more real, more memorable, more significant."

—*The Sunday Oklahoman*

continued . . .

"Wheeler's depiction of life's seemingly random disbursements of joy and sorrow, fulfillment and misery are realistic and gripping. Wheeler delivers an entertaining lesson in how to mine happiness from the dross of disappointment and broken dreams." —*Publishers Weekly*

"Wheeler is a genius of structure and form."
—*El Paso Herald-Post*

"A legal thriller in western clothing, a novel as exciting as anything John Grisham ever wrote. *The Witness* is a page-turner you won't want to put down." —*Roundup Magazine*

"Wheeler is among the two or three top living writers of western historicals—if not the best."
—*Kirkus Reviews*

Cutthroat Gulch

Richard S. Wheeler

SIGNET
Published by New American Library, a division of
Penguin Putnam Inc., 375 Hudson Street,
New York, New York 10014, U.S.A.
Penguin Books Ltd, 80 Strand,
London WC2R 0RL, England
Penguin Books Australia Ltd, 250 Camberwell Road,
Camberwell, Victoria 3124, Australia
Penguin Books Canada Ltd, 10 Alcorn Avenue,
Toronto, Ontario, Canada M4V 3B2
Penguin Books (N.Z.) Ltd, Cnr Rosedale and Airborne Roads,
Albany, Auckland 1310, New Zealand

Penguin Books Ltd, Registered Offices:
Harmondsworth, Middlesex, England

First published by Signet, an imprint of New American Library,
a division of Penguin Putnam Inc.

First Printing, April 2003
10 9 8 7 6 5 4 3 2

Printed in the United States of America

For Elmer Kelton,
with admiration

Chapter 1

Sheriff Blue Smith's fishing hole was one of the privileges of office. They didn't pay him much, so he figured the fishing hole was his, and only his, and he let the world know it.

Let some fool try to fish there and Blue Smith growled and threatened until the wretch left. Everyone in town knew enough to steer clear of Blue's fishing hole, but sometimes a stranger wandered in, and then Blue had to educate him.

It wasn't that Blue owned the place; it was all public land. But Blue had put his brand to it, and that was that. If anyone horned in, Blue found good excuses to haul him before Abe Winters, the JP, or tongue-lash the trespasser until he was scared witless. So they all learned to leave the cutthroat trout to Blue.

Blue figured he'd earned it. He had been sheriff ever since the place had become a county. He'd seen the mountains flush with gold miners, seen wild camps spring up and die, seen crooks and road agents steal from miners when the miners weren't stealing from one another. He had kept the lid on, and now the miners were mostly gone. It was all quiet ranching country, and some day soon the territory would become a state.

That earned Blue his fishing hole and a dozen more like it. The cutthroat trout were heavy, firm fleshed and sweet tasting, especially when the fillets were fried over a campfire. The fish swam in icy snowmelt from the high country, fed on caddis flies, and lurked in the shadows. They put up a fight, and Blue sometimes lost one, which suited him fine.

He had monopolized that fishing hole for more than a quarter of a century and knew every shrub and rock. He knew all its moods and had seen it in every hour, from the blackness of midnight to high noon. He had seen it in dawn mist and in evening dusk. He had seen it when the mountains were purple, when ice topped them, when the pine boughs bent under snow. He had seen it when magpies flocked and wolverines tried to steal his catch.

That's why, on this fine summer afternoon, he noticed at once when he rode down the long forest trail to his hole that he had a visitor dressed in black. This one was sleeping near the bank, exactly where Blue loved to whip his line back and forth and let it sail into the quiet water just below the ripples.

It was probably someone drifting through. If the bum didn't take a hint, Blue would pinch him for vagrancy; that would show the punk a thing or two.

Blue, in no hurry, steered his gelding, Hector, down the pine-girt trail toward the splash of meadow and stream below. Pushing a horse fast down a steep trail is a recipe for trouble, and Blue wasn't looking for trouble on this day. The trespasser was asleep anyway, sprawled on his back and soaking up the sun.

Blue chose Hector for the horse's name because not since the beginning of creation had any horse been named Hector, and that was reason enough. Some overeducated fool in Blankenship, the county seat, had told him that to hector was to swagger and berate. Blue had cussed the fellow out, but secretly was delighted to have a swaggering nag.

He burst at last out of the woods and into the verdant meadow, warmed by a halcyon sun and cooled by a pine-scented breeze. He rode toward the interloper, sourly rehearsing what he would say to the snoring fool. Blue finally arrived at his favorite place in all the world.

The trespasser was dead.

"Well, damn it," Blue Smith said, peering down at a male he had never set eyes on before, a man in a tidy black suit who was staring open-eyed at the sun. A man with one, two, three, four, five, six bullet holes in him, variously piercing his chest, abdomen, neck, and cheek.

A dead trespasser.

Sheriff Smith eased off his mount, squinted at the surrounding black forests and green meadows, eyed the blue peaks, studied the dazzle of light off the water, looked for someone, anyone, and then huddled over the stranger, reading the story. Six shots. Someone had emptied a full six-gun. Blue rolled the body over, looking for bullet holes in the earth, but found none. The corpse had been dragged here, but killed somewhere else.

Blue realized, even as he rolled the man over, that the body was warm. Warm! He gingerly pressed a hand to the man's neck, cheek, hand. Warm. This man had lived and breathed within the hour. But here he was. No sign of rigor mortis. Not yet, anyway.

Smith tugged out the man's pants pockets and found them empty. The suit coat yielded nothing. The black boots were scuffed but serviceable. Not even a ring on a finger. The man's limp hands were too rough for a cardsharp; too smooth for a farmer or rancher. A city man.

Blue felt grief, as he always did, at the sight of violent death. Pity. Some poor devil's life was gone, and the man was not yet thirty. Some mother's son. Maybe some woman's husband. Maybe some child's father. Some mean and miserable skunk had shot this man, and by God, that skunk was going to hang for it.

Smith rose warily, suddenly aware that the killer might still lurk nearby. His revolver rested in one saddlebag. His ham and cheese sandwich, prepared by Olivia, filled the other. His bamboo fly rod rode in the rifle scabbard, as it always did. A yellow rain slicker was tied behind the cantle.

He half expected a shot to rip out of the dark woods and fell him beside the dead man. Blue eased toward Hector, who stood obediently, and fumbled the saddle bag open. The revolver lay naked within. He had not brought his holster or belt or any spare cartridges. This was to be a trout-fishing expedition, not a murder investigation.

He itched to follow the clear trail of the killer: bent grasses, bits of blood, hoof prints. Jump the son of a gun, haul him in, charge him. But Blue knew better. Twenty-nine years of lawing had learned him a few things, and the most important was not to rush off half-cocked. He did track a few hundred yards, right to the edge of the lodgepole pines, but found nothing but a faint crush of grass and specks of blood that were attracting moths. The trail plunged into thick forest in the direction of Pilot Peak, or more likely the saddle between Pilot and Grant Peak. He would return later. He knew as much as he needed to know for the moment.

He had to take this body back to Blankenship and see who could identify it. If he knew the name of the victim, the chances were very good that he would soon know the name of the killer—and save himself a long, hard chase through a vast wilderness. He settled on his favorite ledge over the water, which was so crystal this day, so bright with sun, that the dazzle blinded him. But he wanted to think and watch the dark whirl of trout in the depths. He would be fishing for a killer this time.

Six shots, five probably mortal. Angry killer. Why was the victim dragged here, of all places? Who even knew of this place? Where was this man murdered? Blue rubbed his weatherworn neck and came to no conclusions at all.

Take the dead man to town, that was next. Roll the body into the yellow slicker, tie it to Hector, and walk six miles. Murder had wrecked the afternoon. Wrecked the best fishing in the world. Profaned his favorite place in all of creation. Just for that, the killer should have the privilege of hanging twice.

Blue untied his yellow poncho, spread it, lifted the victim into it, and rolled it up. He carried the dead man easily. Sheriff Blue Smith wasn't particularly large, but he had a lumberjack's shoulders, and many was the miner or crook who had discovered what a wallop he packed in those massive shoulders and arms.

Hector shied away, wild-eyed.

"Whoa, whoa," Blue growled as he slid the yellow-wrapped body over the sidestepping horse. It was going to be a long hike. Blue hated walking, which set his bunions to howling, and the killer was going to pay for this foot-mauling hike along with everything else, including a lost fishing trip on a perfect day.

A two-hour, aching-leg walk. Grimly, Blue led the burdened horse up to the low divide and then down the long, shadowy wooded trail to town. He held the reins in one hand and his Peacemaker in the other, feeling foolish about it. He could just as well put the iron back into the saddlebag for all the good it did him.

He had fished that hole all these years and had never seen it profaned. He had brought his boy, Absalom, there, and taught him to cast. Brought his girl, Tamara, too, and let her clean the trout and cook them for him; make herself capable. She turned out fine; married a rancher down the valley.

The boy never took to the West—or fishing or hunting or even the territory—and finally skipped out, wanting something Blue couldn't give him. Absalom wasn't man enough for the territory. Last Blue knew, the boy was an engraver for some magazine in Denver. An *artist*. Blue hawked up some saliva and spat.

Blue knew exactly what he would do in town. He would leave the body with Vinegar Will, who styled himself the Maestro of Mortuary Arts, and would warn him not to touch it. Then he'd get the coroner, Doc Prentiss. Blue would tell his deputy, Carl Barlow, to fetch every saloon keeper in town; one or another of the barkeeps in the thirteen saloons of Blankenship should recognize the stranger. Get Cyrus Mack, the editor of the *Blankenship Weekly Crier*, too. Newspaper editors meet everyone. Then Blue'd get a John Doe warrant from District Judge Nils Berdinger and see who knew the victim.

Then he would decide whether to hunt down the killer or wait for him to return to town.

Young Carl Barlow was a good enough man, but his experience would fit into a thimble. He'd never dealt with a dangerous man because there hadn't been any in Blankenship for seven or eight years. Each election Barlow ran against Blue Smith and lost, which was fine with Blue. The county supervisors wanted Blue to retire and always pushed for a Barlow victory. So did the editor of the weekly. Old Smith was too rough, too hard, too stubborn, too single-minded, and maybe he'd been around too long and the pioneer days were over, they said, but Blue had laughed at that.

He was rough, all right, and he intended to stay in office until they carried him out feet first. And then some lucky cuss would get his fishing hole.

He arrived at last in Blankenship and led the burdened horse through back streets toward Vinegar's Gateway to Heaven Chapel, which had the only white Corinthian columns in town. People stared, but a glower from Blue kept them at bay.

"Vinegar," he bellowed, at the rear door.

"I wish you wouldn't call me that," the mortician said.

"Lay this man out and don't touch him. You'll be having visitors in a few minutes."

Blue carried the stiffening yellow burden through the back door of the establishment and laid him down on a copper-jacketed mortician's table.

Vinegar gave the body a clucking and sniffling professional appraisal, and slid Blue's poncho out from under it.

"Who is he?" he asked.

"We'll find out," Blue said.

"Unknown male. Potter's field," Vinegar said, pursing his lips in the manner that won him his name.

"Maybe not. He doesn't look poor to me. And he's going to be known soon."

Vinegar began tugging at the victim's pockets.

"I've already looked," Blue said.

"Pity," Vinegar said. Blue wondered what he meant by that.

Blue rode Hector over to the shabby sheriff's office, which squatted around the back of the courthouse, hidden from public view by the county fathers, who didn't want to admit to the existence of crime in this Eden.

He wrapped Hector's reins around the hitchrail and entered the cool gloom. Barlow was fishing something out of the brass spittoon, and sat up violently.

"Didn't expect you," he muttered.

"We've had a murder."

"A murder!" Barlow straightened up, startled. "Who?"

"Stranger. I want you to have a look. He's at Vinegar's. Then round up anyone who can identify him. Saloon men."

"We haven't had a murder in ten, twelve years, Blue."

"Six bullet holes, Carl. Five fatal wounds. I found him at the fishing hole. Fresh killed, still warm."

"Motive?"

"Don't know for sure."

"Robbed?"

"Yes; not a thing on him. But why would a robber unload a whole cylinder? There's more here."

Barlow grabbed a holster belt and hung it from his skinny waist. Blankenship was so peaceful that no law man bothered to wear sidearms; billy clubs sufficed.

"This'll start an uproar, Blue."

Blue agreed. "It's the first one since that drunken brawl in 1880. And the last."

Chapter 2

Blue watched them file through. Saloon men like Mike Solomon and Gad York studied the dead man and shook their heads.

"Never seen 'im before," Dinty Jones said.

Maybe Cyrus Mack would know. The editor peered over his spectacles, moved the lamp around to light shadowed areas, frowned, and shook his head. "Nope," he said. And then he pulled out his notepad. "Where'd you find him?"

"Later," Blue snapped.

"The public has a right to know."

"You'll know plenty soon enough." Blue relented. "I found an unidentified body out of town. Six bullet wounds. Male, about thirty. There's your story."

"Where?"

"I ain't saying."

"You could cooperate, you know."

"I could, but I won't." Blue thought maybe the place where he found the body might mean something, and he wasn't ready to reveal it.

"I'm hanging around here until he's identified."

"Suit yourself."

Blue had Barlow round up the three preachers in Blankenship, who nervously examined the remains and shook their heads.

"Not in my congregation," said the Reverend Mr. Albright.

"All right, thank you," Blue said, hustling the divine out the door.

He was out of leads, and the trail was getting cold. If you knew who the killer was, or even why the crime happened, no trail ever grew cold. But now he faced a cold trail and the killer had a good lead.

"You done?" asked Vinegar.

"No, I'm not. I'm getting Bart Fly in here. You fix up the dead man."

"You mean, like he wasn't shot?"

"His face, Vinegar, his face. Open his eyes and spread some putty on that cheek. Like he's alive."

Ten minutes later Fly was focusing his camera lens on the propped-up remains.

"Give me front and profile pictures, Bart. And then make me ten tintypes. Give them to Barlow and bill the county."

The photographer, whose head bobbed

under the black shroud of his equipment, nodded. A flash of magnesium powder blinded Blue. The shutter clicked.

"I'll have them in a week, sheriff."

"Tomorrow."

"That's impossible."

"Tomorrow."

Fly sighed. "You're the stubbornest man I ever met. I'll be up all night. I should charge double."

Magnesium powder exploded again as a shutter clicked. Acrid smoke filtered past the lamp.

"All right, Vinegar, he's yours," Blue said. "One more thing: Look for scars. I want a sketch of every scar and every bullet hole. I want entrance and exit holes figured out. You find anything unusual, you let Barlow know pronto."

"I hope I get paid."

"So do I."

Blue pulled his battered hat from his head and stood over the dead man. "I'm sorry," he said. "A man has a right to dignity. Man only dies once. Whoever you are, I'll see about some justice. Notify your kin."

He memorized that face.

Blue turned to Barlow. "I'm going after the killer. Ride down that trail he left. I know where it goes. It'll take a while. The office is all yours. We've a few leads; put them to use while I'm gone. When you get a tintype, check with the hostlers in town. Try the hotel clerks. Try the restaurants. Send one image to the Centerville marshal and see if Zeke Dombrowski knows something. Try every merchant here—grocers, feed store. Don't forget to talk to little boys; they see stuff. Put a hundred-dollar reward ad in the paper. I'll square it with the county."

"You going alone?"

"Posses are a pain in the ass."

Barlow grinned. "You want him for yourself."

"You bet I do."

"How long?"

"Long as it takes."

"Blue, give me some idea."

"If it takes me the rest of my life, then that's what I'll spend."

"Why you so het up?"

"My fishing hole, that's why."

Barlow laughed, but Blue didn't see anything funny about it.

"I'm sending a rescue outfit after you in one week. Where are you going?"

"I don't know."

"Blue, dammit."

"The trail leads toward that saddle between Pilot and Grant peaks."

Barlow nodded. "I'll come lookin'."

Blue watched Vinegar Will mash the stiff body onto the copper table again and fold the hands across the man's breast. Vinegar always hummed his way through his labors, and on this occasion it was "The Battle Hymn of the Republic," where the grapes of wrath are stored.

"Carl, I want a fancy funeral for this gent. Put a notice in the paper. See who comes. Write down the names. Vinegar, you put out a guest book. I want to know who signs it."

"Do you figure he's Protestant, Catholic, or heathen?" Vinegar asked.

"Anyone who gets shot must be a heathen."

"You like to spread blame where it don't belong, Blue."

"Some of it sticks," Blue said.

Blue Smith figured he had done all the damage he could, and so he headed for home. He lived on Parcel Street, two blocks away from the courthouse and the sheriff's office. He collected Hector, rolled up his slicker and tied it to the cantle, and swung aboard stiffly. The complaint of his body reminded him of his long walk and the ordeal to come.

He put the gelding into his carriage barn, unsaddled it, brushed and fed it, and poured a pail of oats into the manger. He pumped a few buckets of water into the trough, and then headed for the weathered gray clapboard cottage that had been his nest for half a lifetime.

He found Olivia glaring from her blind eyes.

"Late again; cold chow. Sit your butt and eat cold."

"Murder," he said.

"No, I don't intend to go that far, but pretty near," she said.

"Found a body."

"You did, did you? Whose dog?"

"No, a body, at the fishing hole. Six bullet holes in it."

She paused at last. "Anyone we know?"

"Stranger."

"Why there?"

"That's what I ask myself."

"Someone wanted you to see it there."

"Aw, Olivia."

She abandoned the wood stove and found him with her hands. "Someone wanted you to find it there. Someone who knows about that place . . . and you."

Blue found her hand. Ever since cataracts had squeezed the sight from her eyes, Olivia had acquired an uncanny sixth sense. And Blue had learned to heed it.

"What was he like?" she asked.

"Thirties, dark complected, black suit, groomed, nothing in any pocket."

"So young."

"Young and unknown in these parts."

"What are going to do?"

"Go after him."

She nodded and returned easily to her serving. He marveled that she could live as she did, almost as if she could see. She could discern light and shadow, knew night from ivory daylight. Sometimes she said her days were like living inside a pearl. Somehow she knew where things were, knew how to cope with the wood range, even keep the fire going. She knew how close to put her hand to a hot kettle, knew how to wash a dish spotless clean, even though she could see nothing of it.

Now she ladled beef stew into a bowl, spilling not a drop, and brought it to him.

"When?" she asked.

"Soon as I can load up."

"I thought so. When will you be back? Foolish damned question."

He had no answer for her. He would follow the trail until he caught his man. The stew was a marvel. How did she manage to salt it just right? She couldn't even see her saltcellar.

"You be all right? I'll have Barlow check on you."

"I will need stove kindling."

"That all?"

She shrugged. The shrug meant that the longer he took, the more she would need help. He hated like hell to leave her. He could leave in the morning; spend the evening getting her squared away. But he wouldn't. He wanted to camp this night at the fishing hole and start on that trail at dawn. He wanted to wake up with his senses howling at him, the old hunting instinct commanding his every thought.

"I'll send word to Tamara," he said. "She can come in for a while."

Olivia didn't object. Tamara was their married daughter, Mrs. Steven Cooper, who lived on a ranch beyond Centerville. Olivia had named both children, Tamara and Absalom, names Blue had always found odd. Blue had started life named David, and Olivia said that Tamara and Absalom were children of the biblical king. No one had called Blue by his given name in thirty years, and if anyone did, it would fetch a snarl from him. He couldn't even remember why he was called Blue; maybe it was because his black hair had a blue cast to it. He preferred to think it was because he was profane.

Blue told Olivia the whole story as he spooned the stew: finding the body, six shots, hauling it in, trying for some identification.

"It was someone the killer didn't care about," she said.

"No, it was someone the killer hated so much he emptied his six-gun."

"Didn't care about," she said.

He started to grumble but checked it.

He spent the next hour putting together his kit. He had done this many times and knew exactly what he needed. He would take a pack horse even if it slowed him down. Speed rarely mattered in a manhunt. You get a sense of the quarry, you begin to understand, and you keep on, and sooner or later you catch up. That's when a good kit comes in handy: beans for two, manacles, spare tack, a good pair of blankets, a ground cloth.

Even as he collected his gear, Olivia was putting together his chow: beans, parched corn, some ground Arbuckles, some potatoes and onions, some tins of tomatoes.

He hefted his Winchester lever action rifle and realized he wouldn't take it. His eyes weren't so good anymore. A man passes fifty and things go to hell. With the way people mumbled, Blue sometimes needed an ear trumpet and he couldn't read a word without his wire-rimmed spectacles. A scattergun would be handier; you just pointed, not aimed. Maybe there were several killers, not just one. The killer was no doubt male, but Blue had just better keep his mind open on that score. A woman could pull a trigger just as well as a man, even if the gun bucked worse against her shoulder.

His double-barreled Browning, then, and some double-ought buckshot. His Peacemaker revolver. His one set of leg irons. Manacles. He laid it all out on the battered kitchen table, along with two boxes of .45 caliber brass shells.

Then he threw a packsaddle and panniers over his nitwitted yawning mule, saddled Hector, and loaded up in the twilight.

He found Olivia doing dishes, and turned her into his arms.

"You be good," he said.

"Not if I can help it."

He laughed. She not only said it whenever he left town, but she also meant it. Whenever he returned, there would be a new story or two about her floating around town. When he left, she took it as permission for a fling. Once Barlow had carefully carried her home after relieving her of a brandy bottle. Another time Barlow had hauled Olivia out of Bessie May's parlor. God only knows what that was about.

It was full dark when he was ready. He slipped into the creaking saddle, took one last glance at the shadowed cottage and his old gal in the open door, and rode into the night, the hoof sounds hollow in the hush.

Chapter 3

Hector knew the way. Blue gave him his head and sat back in the creaking saddle. The old mule followed behind, keeping the lead rope slack.

Blue had often ridden Hector to his fishing hole at night because Blue liked to cast his first line before dawn, when the day was merely a blue promise in the east. That's when mists rose from the river and dew coated every blade, and he could feel the glory of the world being born. Maybe it was ownership. If he was there, as dawn patrolled the east, he owned that hole for that day.

He topped the divide and worked downslope through the forest. Far to the west the sky lit and quieted, and a faint rumble echoed its way to him; thunderstorm over there. But straight above, the sky was clear and black, the stars at a distance beyond imagining.

Blue reckoned it was not yet midnight when he rode softly into the place. He smelled rain on the eddies of chilled air flowing down from the high country and wished he had packed a shelter cloth. Cumbersome thing for a manhunt, but not a bad idea when poking around eleven-thousand-foot slopes in a bone-chilling rain, or when trapped in a summer mountain blizzard.

He tugged the gear off the horse and mule and picketed them on lush meadow grass. The old hidey-hole felt different this time, violated by manslaughter. Blue avoided the spot beside the fishing hole where he had found the body, and settled down beside a thicket of whispering aspen. He scraped the sticks and pebbles away, unrolled his India rubberized ground cloth, pulled his canvas panniers up for a head-rest, and wrapped himself in the blankets. He would not sleep easily; he never did out of doors when a part of him was listening for a bear or a coyote or a storm. But the lack of rest rarely bothered him unless he was out for five or six days in a row.

He got up, withdrew the scattergun from its scabbard, and tucked it into the blankets, feeling comforted but not knowing why. That killer would be twenty miles away by now.

Grizzly, he said to himself, but he had never seen a grizzly just there, or seen any grizzly scat, and a scatter gun would not be the weapon of choice.

He stared at the heavens, wishing that he could plumb the mysteries of the world. An unknown man had been murdered nearby by an unknown killer; he could make no sense of it. Sometimes in the past he had been able to crawl inside the mind of the criminal and calculate how to catch the man. Maybe he would this time. People had habits. People had a way of dealing with wilderness. An abandoned campsite could tell a tale.

Just before he left, Olivia had touched his bristly cheek, her fingers ever so tender as they limned his face and the gray stubble. She saw the world through her fingers now, but that wasn't why she touched him. She was saying a thousand things to him, and most of all, *Be careful, love. Be very careful.*

A dozen times over the years he had been a sheriff, she had waited for him, not knowing, for days and nights. And once when they had carried him into the cottage, his chest wrapped in bloody sheets, she had screamed. Now she would be waiting again, and for a lawman slowed down by the weight of years, a man who stubbornly rode alone just when he should be forming a posse, just because he took crime as a personal affront.

Twice during the night he bolted up and grabbed his shotgun. Once it was nothing. The other time he felt rather than saw a deer leap away. He heard a cutthroat trout break the surface and fall back. He felt foolish. Somewhere out there, putting miles between this place and himself, was a killer.

Blue knew dawn was near from the sharp, wet cold and the ache in his bones, so he stood up. By the time he could see the slopes, he would be ready to travel. He pulled on his ice-cold boots and slid the scattergun back into its sheath. He wrapped his cold holster and belt around his bulging waist and was ready for the day. He debated a breakfast fire and some Arbuckles coffee, and decided to go ahead.

The kindling was wet and didn't want to catch, and then smoked coldly after Blue added some fire-starter scraped from the underside of cottonwood bark. But Blue knew the flame would win out, and he dug into his possibles for the Arbuckles, which Olivia had ground up and poured into a Harvest Maid cracker tin. He filled the old speckled blue pot with ice water from the river, added some coffee, and set it to heating. Soon a low layer of wood smoke drifted across the meadow.

He eyed his horse and mule. They stood looking at him, not away, which was a good sign. He was going deaf; they weren't. He had learned to watch their ears, read their preoccupation.

He poured some rolled oats into his iron skillet, added water, stirred them, and set them to heating. He drifted out to the meadows to collect his horse and mule, which stood like statues, radiating their own heat. That's when he saw the straw hat. The gloom was so thick he scarcely recognized it, but sure enough, it was a hat. A wide-brimmed woman's hat, bright with a silky pink band that pierced through slits at either side and formed long streamers that could be tied under the chin. It sure looked familiar.

The hat was dew-damped. Blue turned it around in his hand, amazed by its presence. Why hadn't he seen it yesterday? Because he was so absorbed with death, that's why. But surely he would have seen it. How could he not see it? How did it get there? He returned to the fire so he could get a better look. Good straw hat. The dead man had a wife, perhaps. Or daughter. Where was she? Were there more bodies here? Was she the killer? Was there more to this than murder? Rape, abduction, family trouble? He would take the hat with him; someone might recognize it.

He added a pinch of salt to his gruel and ate it slowly, straight out of the hot skillet, as he waited for his coffee to cool. The trout were breakfasting, rising up and out and sliding back so quietly it took a sharp eye to spot them. Why the hell had he come here without a pole? He could have had trout instead of a mouthful of sticky oats.

Did she fish? Did he fish? Were they here because it was the likeliest hole on the river? Blue finished, sipped his java, admiring the strong tang of Arbuckle's best, and washed out the pot and the spoon in the river.

The light had stolen in while he ate, still purple and lavender. Now he could look around. He rose stiffly, the night's hard bed still remembered by his bones, and walked to the place where he had found the body—until yesterday his favorite place, just over the quiet deep waters of the hole. He found nothing new. No purse or wallet. No signs of struggle. He patrolled in a widening circle, round and round the meadow, looking for another body—a woman's—but he found nothing more.

Time to go. He doused the fire, packed his gear, loaded the animals, and rode through the meadow, following the plain trail of a dragged body, broken grass, the scrape of a boot, and those flecks of brown that he knew were human blood. The place of execution would not be far away.

The trail plunged into the still night-bound woods, and now the trail was even plainer. Scuffed pine needles marked the passage. He struck a place where gray granite vaulted up from the river bottoms, and there, suddenly, his horse nickered and another horse reciprocated. Surprised, Blue slid out his revolver, studied the gloom, and discerned an animal ahead. But no man. He waited a minute, uneasy and quick on the trigger, and then eased his horse forward into a small brush-choked clearing walled by a cliff. A handsome copper-colored bay horse stood there, tied to a tree with a stout rope. Its head hung low. Blue knew at once it was suffering from the want of water and feed, and had been there for some while.

The dead man's horse: handsome, with black stockings, a groomed mane and tail, and a torso sleek with coppery summer hair.

"Whoa," Blue said, still not trusting the place. He studied the dark and silent woods, seeing nothing. He slid off Hector and approached the tied horse. It jittered back, testing the picket line, which was tied to an aspen.

"Whoa, boy," Blue muttered. He walked slowly around the wild-eyed animal, looking for a brand and finding none. Gingerly, wary of a kick, Blue ran a hand over the animal's thigh muscle, looking for a haired-over mark. Nothing. Eastern horse, then. Maybe fifteen hands. Some Thoroughbred in him. Good dished head, almost Arab. Not a stocky Western animal; no mustang blood. Worth plenty. Brought by rail from some long distance away. It all fit: the right horse for a man in a black suit. Almost a flashy horse, with speed in him. And now it was desperate for a drink and some feed. Blue slid a hand down a foreleg and lifted it. Fresh shoe, no cleat on it. Gently he tried a rear leg. Same sort of shoe, no cleat. He could read those hoofprints.

Blue considered. He didn't need the horse. Let him go. The animal would head for the river and stay there at the fishing hole, where there was plenty of grass and a good meadow. Catch him later, take him back to Blankenship. Someone might recognize that animal.

The horse had tugged the knot at the aspen so tight that Blue could not loosen it, and he finally cut the rope with his Barlow knife. Then he unbuckled the halter. The bay stood.

"Go," Blue said, slapping the horse.

It squealed, snorted, and ran downslope toward the water. Blue sighed. He was not done with this gloomy place. He studied the dark woods uneasily and headed for the wall of granite that rose abruptly just ahead. The light was thickening above; the sky had turned bold blue. The sun had not yet pierced this mountain valley, and wouldn't for a while.

He found what he was looking for almost immediately: two white pocks chest level in the granite, and two more lower down. The last of the shots from the six-gun followed the dying man as he slid to the ground. Brown splashes on the pine needles and grass at the foot. Scuffed turf. Only minutes before Blue had arrived at the fishing hole the day before, murder had been done here; cold, calculating, brutal. An execution. He saw design in it, not passion; cold murder, not anger. He thought he knew even less about the killer than before.

He looked for prints but found none that were legible in the pine-needle carpet. No clear hoof prints, no clear boot heels. No women's shoes or boots.

Blue stood quietly and let the place speak to him, but learned nothing more. This place was evil; he felt the darkness of it there. He was only a quarter of a mile from his fishing hole, but he had never been just here. His boy probably had. Absalom had never had the patience to fish, and wandered the little basin as if it were a cage while Blue cast for cutthroats. The boy's name was too much of a mouthful, so they called him Jinx. He didn't like that, either, but it stuck until Absalom was in his teen years and insisted on being called by his given name. What sort of honest-to-God male didn't like to fish? Jinx never did, and it irritated Blue to this day. Raise a kid in paradise, and all he could think of was the bright gaslights of the nearest city. Blue waited a moment longer, but this grim place wasn't whispering to him, and it was time to move along.

He wasn't even sure where the trail led because the horses of the killer and victim had trod on pine needles. It would be a guess. Blue clambered onto his gelding and headed toward the ridge high above, hoping to pick up the trail there. What if the killer had come from that direction and left by another?

There was no way to know, not just then.

Half of tracking was reading the land. Nature was always forcing living things to go one way or another, and people acted much the same as animals when it came to flat ground, obstacles, slopes, fording a river, or dodging danger.

Blue headed upslope, following a drainage that led to that saddle miles above. The woods told him nothing, but after an hour of labored climbing he emerged on a sloping meadow that was brightly clad in the morning sun and rioting with purple and yellow wildflowers, so that he felt he was walking up a rainbow. He could never remember the names of half the damned things.

Here were signs of passage, like crushed pasqueflowers and hoofprints in the moist earth. He paused to study them. A single horse, heavily laden, judging from the depth of its prints, was heading into the high country. Blue wove left and right, looking for other prints, especially those of the bay. But the stranger had come from some other direction, and so had the killer. These prints were larger than those of the bay, and this big horse had carried the killer away from the fishing hole.

He could not tell how old the prints were. For all of his years in this wild land, he had never quite mastered the subtleties of reading sign. If a print was dried out and hard and blurred, it was old; if sharp and in moist ground, it was probably fresh. That's as much as Blue could manage. But he was damned if he would hire some drunken scout to advise him.

At a plateau Blue paused to let Hector and the mule blow. They had climbed six or eight hundred feet above the fishing hole, and the view was grand. From up here he could look down on the Wilson River, glinting its way through the secluded valley, and off to the west he could see the snow-shrouded blue peaks of the high country, Grant and Sherman and Terry, which guarded this vast green land and nurtured it with their water.

Puffball clouds hung on the highest peaks, looking more innocent than they were. A cow elk and her new calf stood quietly, watching Blue. The sight of all that was enough to make a man forget he was hunting down a killer. But not for long.

Chapter 4

Blue worked quietly upslope, not worried about running into his quarry, who was a day ahead. The prints of a single horse led steadily away from the fishing hole, through timber and meadow, past talus, into rushing freshets, around dense thickets of new-leafed aspen.

The killer was not pushing his horse. Every little while he had stopped, rested the animal, and let it graze while he did his chores. Blue found some boot prints; round toe, worn heels, medium sized, not much different from his own boots, but wider.

Blue thought maybe he was gaining. The killer didn't know he was being followed. If he didn't have a pack horse, he wasn't far from home, and everything he needed hung from his pommel or was stowed behind his cantle.

What sort of man was he? One who was comfortable in nature. Blue found the remains of a small fire, compact and tucked into a corner of rock, safe from the wind—a site that made a natural stove where a man could boil some water or cook a meal. Blue could tell at a glance that the man enjoyed the outdoors, and he approved. Blue filed away the knowledge, knowing that it might prove useful.

At each place where the man had dismounted, Blue searched the whole area, looking for a cache, for a spent brass shell, for evidence of any sort. He found nothing at all.

Blue pushed ahead, keeping a weather eye on the peaks, which generated their own storms. But so far this June day glowed with sunlight. He passed blue spruce and Engelmann pines, lodgepole thickets so dense a man on foot couldn't penetrate them, a place where fire had scoured the slope. He found bear scratches on one of the pines, and decided it was time to watch out for Old Ephriam.

Blue passed parks bursting with purple larkspur or blue flax, stands of alder and birch. He didn't need to follow the hoofprints; the rising country was hemming him in, and there was only one way to go. If this weren't a manhunt, he would be enjoying a glorious day, with zephyrs mixing warm and chill air, the scent of pines heavy, the air so fresh and sweet that he sucked in lungfuls just for the sheer pleasure of it.

He followed a chattering creek upward,

through dark timber that hid the peaks above. He skirted a huge blowdown, where some violent force of nature had flattened thousands of trees and torn limbs off others, heaping them all into kindling. The mountains were rarely benign; they sprang at a man darkly, killed and mauled plant and animal alike.

Sometimes he found hoofprints. Most often he didn't, but that was not important. He rode alone, a solitary man, content with the world, not a bit lonely, the natural wonders at hand substituting for conversation.

Maybe Carl Barlow was making progress; maybe the dead man had a name now. Maybe someone had been reported missing, someone from Centerville on the other side of the county or someplace where Blue didn't know many people. Maybe Barlow would catch the suspect and have him in the lockup when Blue returned.

That was all right.

He wondered how Olivia was doing. She would have her toot and there would be no stopping her. When the cat was away, he thought, that pretty little mouse would play. There would be a few stories floating around: Olivia taking a nip, Olivia cussing a butcher with words that never passed her lips when Blue was in town.

It made him uneasy sometimes. What kind of woman was the one Olivia kept hidden from

Blue? What had she taught the children? But mostly he just laughed. If Olivia wanted a nip or wanted to cast aside her churchy inhibitions, then he'd just keep quiet. Hell, he'd lived with Olivia for thirty years. People used Olivia's toots against him in the elections, but it hadn't cost him any votes, except maybe those of Mrs. Peabody, who ran the temperance society. She had tried to make an issue of Olivia's drinking in the paper, but Cyrus Mack wouldn't print her letter and told Blue so. He said Blue was running for office, not Olivia.

Along the creek bed he followed right on top of the killer's hoofprints because there was no other passage. He glanced ahead at sun-dappled parks, mostly watching out for bear. He feared black bears more than grizzlies, even if they lacked the ferocity of the bigger bear. He didn't know why he harbored all sorts of preferences and prejudices; he just did.

As noon approached he burst out of the thickets into an upland of thin alpine tundra that stretched toward the saddle. Here the landscape changed abruptly; naked gray rock, stunted bristlecone pines twisted by wind, arctic tundra dotted with tiny blooms not even as large as a button. A chill wind sliced into his coat, and he pulled up the collar. June it might be down in Blankenship; up here it was March.

The huge peaks rose to either side, naked gray rock splashed with decaying snowbanks, harboring little life except the pikas sunning themselves and an occasional coyote. He saw an eagle hanging in the sky.

When he topped the saddle he rode over a broad hump for a hundred yards, with gravel and tundra underfoot. And then, suddenly, the other side of the slopes opened before him, a vast sea of mountain and forest lost in haze a hundred miles distant. He tugged the reins and stared. He had never been up here before, on the roof of the world.

Down there somewhere to the south, but not in sight, was Centerville. It too had started as a mining town, mostly silver but some gold and copper too, and when the pockets of ore gave out it turned into a shopping town for the local ranches, a quarter of the size it had been at the peak of its boom. Down that valley to the southwest, beyond what he could see, was Tamara's place. She and her husband Steve raised fat red shorthorns on a well-watered flat surrounded by verdant hills that stretched higher and higher into the high country. Blue thought maybe he might have a chance to stop in. The killer had been drifting toward Centerville, and that was enough of a clue. Blue would have a talk with Zeke Dombrowski, the town constable.

Blue let the horse and mule blow; the last half mile had been steep. The wind cut sharply through his clothing, and he was eager to start down the long grade and into that line of firs below. Maybe he'd have himself a lunch, if he could get out of the wind.

He felt the shot before he heard it. The gelding shuddered, stood rigidly, and then started to cave, even as a sharp snap racketed through the air. He felt his horse weaken and weave, and he pulled his right foot loose of the stirrup just as the animal dropped to the left. He hit the ground violently, banged his head, and landed on his revolver and pain shot through his hip. The horse collapsed on Blue's left leg, pinning him under it. Fiery pain bloomed in his leg.

He heard another shot, and then the squeal of the mule. He heard his mule struggle and collapse. Then he heard nothing.

He was helpless. Fear engulfed him. He raged at himself for being so careless. But most of all he wanted to live, and he didn't know whether he would last one more minute with that killer a hundred yards away.

He tried to move his pinned leg. He tried to pull his shotgun from its scabbard, but it, too, lay under the horse. He felt Hector slump into death with a last sigh, heavier on his leg now. His good horse, sixteen years his friend, dead in a few seconds. In death Hcetor was performing one last service to Blue, shielding him from the muzzle of that gun down below.

He half expected a dark form to fill the sky above him and struggled to reach his revolver.

Every time he moved, his bruised hip howled. He felt blood on his temple, where it had struck rock. He crabbed sideways and found that he could pull his leg, inch by inch, out from under the horse. The leg felt broken. He ignored the pain, or at least endured it, as he tugged his leg bit by bit. His holster bit at him, and he managed to undo his belt and let the holster twist away.

Fear shot through him. Dead animals, maybe a broken leg, and maybe a killer even now stalking up that grade, ready to dispatch him. He tugged at the holster and got it free. He worked his revolver loose, liking the cold hard heft of it in his hand, the pressure of his finger on the double-action trigger. He peered about, craning to see, armed now, five loads to defend himself. . . . If he didn't faint from the pain.

He could not see the mule, which was hidden by the dead gelding. He needed to get loose, and began once again to pull his leg free, feeling it scrape against rock, feeling his muscles howl with the slightest motion. He was sweating. His heart raced.

He tugged hard, and this time he pulled his leg free. He lay on his back, fearful of the shadow that might suddenly loom above him. But he saw only some puffy clouds and a soaring crow. The wind had coaxed his hat away, just out of reach, and he crabbed toward it, catching it just as it started to slide away again.

He pulled it to him. It was a fine old pearly hat, sweat-stained and comfortable. But now it would serve another purpose. He lacked a stick to lift it, so he gingerly clasped the brim and raised it above the torso of his brown horse, expecting it to be blown from his fingers. But nothing happened. He lifted the hat higher. Nothing happened. The killer was too smart to shoot at a hat, or maybe too close to bother.

Blue lay on the cold rock, fearful, not knowing what to do. Darkness would cloak him eventually, but darkness would come very late this June night. He needed to know if he could walk. He felt along his leg, looking for knots, for broken bones, for torn ligaments. Plenty of pain, more than he had ever known, but he could find no fracture. He might be able to walk. He wouldn't know until he tried.

He crawled toward the head of the horse and peered around it. He could see nothing and he was too low to see who or what was down that slope. Whoever had shot his horse and mule had been an expert. A single bullet to the heart had killed the gelding. Two shots, two dead animals.

It occurred to Blue that the killer could just as easily have killed him, *but didn't*. The killer was toying with him, wanting him to suffer, wanting to put fear into him. And succeeding. Blue knew that he was entirely at the mercy of the man. The killer wasn't a day's ride ahead, as

Blue had supposed, he was maybe a hundred yards ahead, and probably enjoying Blue's terror.

If that was so, then there was only one thing to do. Blue stuffed the revolver into his holster, rolled over, lifted himself on his good leg, and stood up.

Chapter 5

Blue stood, the cold wind whipping him. His right leg hurt but he could stand on it all right. He cradled the shotgun in the crook of his arm and waited. If anyone was coming for him, it would happen soon. But no one came. He limped toward that line of wind-twisted pine where the killer had waited for him, clambered down a steep rocky slope, and felt every step.

The stunted trees a hundred yards below, might tell a story. He plunged into them and soon found the place. Some scuffed dirt and two ejected brass cartridges told him all he needed to know. Forty-four caliber Winchester. He pocketed them. He had the feeling these would not be the first he would be pocketing. He stared upward toward the pass, aware of how perfectly he and his horse and mule had been skylined and what a fool he had been to suppose the killer was twenty miles away.

The trail disappeared into woods below, but he didn't follow it. Instead he worked back to the pass, wincing as his leg rebelled. He figured he had better get used to it, because he had a long walk ahead of him.

On top he tried to pull his riding saddle off his big old horse, but couldn't. He couldn't do much with the pack saddle and panniers on the mule, either. The perpetual wind sailing through that pass chilled him. In the mountains, cold was the enemy. He was six or seven miles—and more than three hours on foot—from the fishing hole, assuming he could walk. He would need to cross several rills and runnels and one good-sized creek, too.

He untied his slicker from its nest behind the cantle and stuffed some shotgun shells into his pockets. He would leave the revolver and cartridge belt here, in one of the panniers. A revolver wasn't worth carrying in this country; it was a good enough city weapon, though. He found an old undershirt and tied it tight around his leg above and below the knee. The binding felt good.

He remembered at last to undo Hector's bridle and reins and bring them with him, along with a halter and lead rope. He stared at the lifeless horse, feeling bad, and removed his hat. He would never hear Hector nicker again. Damned good horse, at least most of the time. They had seen a lot of living together. Blue screwed his hat onto his head. It was one more reason to catch that son of a gun and string him up.

Satisfied that he had what he needed, he started back, down rocky grade and past bristlecone pines, his leg howling at him. But he ignored it. At least it wasn't broken. That would have been his death sentence.

He wore the slicker so he wouldn't have to carry it and let the shotgun ride his shoulder. But the walking tired him, and he hadn't gone two hundred yards before he needed to catch his breath. He was high up; maybe ten thousand feet. But it was the leg pain that wearied him.

Meanwhile the killer was riding away, having succeeded in driving off his pursuer. The whole business puzzled Blue. It was almost as if the killer knew him, knew his habits, knew where he liked to fish, knew when Blue would arrive at the fishing hole and find a warm body, knew what Blue would do, knew where to wait for him. And then shoot his horse and mule rather than shoot the sheriff. Damned if he could figure it out.

Blue knew his knee was swelling; it chafed within his britches and against his binding. But there was nothing he could do. He limped down the long trail, past the blowdown, over a rill, into lodgepole forest. At the roaring creek he hunted for the best way across, found a log to sit on, pulled off his boots and stockings, undid his binding and then his pants, and stepped gingerly into the ice water.

"Damn!" he bellowed, shocked by the numbing cold. He slipped and slid his way across, hurt himself anew clambering up the far bank, and then dressed himself. He was lucky he didn't break his neck. It made a man appreciate a saddle horse.

Late that afternoon Blue stumbled into the fishing hole meadow, and there was the coppery bay, watching him. He set down his shotgun, took off the slicker, and started across the lush grass to catch the bay, but it shied from him every time he approached. His bum leg was hurting all the worse, so he gave up for the moment, headed to his favorite perch overlooking the quiet pool below the rills, and sat down. The water was still. Those big cutthroat wouldn't be biting, not then. Not until dusk. But they were there, lurking in the shadows, dark under the cutbanks, waiting for whatever trout wait for, an occasional flip of the tail keeping them where they liked to live out their watery lives. The warmth made him sleepy. This was a sheltered valley, unlike the raw rock nakedness of that high pass at the shoulder of Grant Peak.

He had a killer to catch, not to mention a horse. He was no further now toward resolving the mystery than he was when he started. He did his best thinking right there, at the fishing hole, and maybe he would come up with something. But this time he had no line to cast, no lures, no bamboo rod.

The bay returned to its grazing, but it was grazing closer, curious about the man at the water's edge. Blue watched and waited. The bay wasn't unfriendly, just uncertain.

One thing was plain: The killer was someone who knew him, or at least had studied his ways. But was the killer someone Blue knew? Blue thought of all the hard cases he had collared, including a dozen who had been sentenced to long terms in the territorial penitentiary. Maybe he was facing one of them. Half swore they would get even some day, and some had tried, only to bounce back behind bars.

But that made little sense now. No one was after him as far as he knew. This whole thing made no sense. He was after a killer; a killer who chose not to kill him when he had the chance, a killer who was warning him off rather than killing him.

Well, he'd get that killer. They all had a way of underestimating old Blue, maybe because Blue didn't put on airs. *There's nothing flashy about old Blue,* he thought. Plain words, plain revolver, plain man in office. Stubborn too. They all told him that, whenever he got his back up and wanted to do things his own way.

He rose, feeling the protest of his twisted knee, and walked slowly toward the bay, which stopped grazing and waited alertly.

"Whoa, boy," Blue said.

The bay let him approach and slide a rein over his black mane. In a moment, Blue had him. He pushed the bit into the bay's mouth and buckled the bridle. It was too tight so he loosened it. He took a rein and walked the horse across the meadow to that wooded place where the stranger had been shot and where Blue had left the bay's saddle. A few minutes later he had the bay blanketed and saddled. The stranger had been taller than Blue, so Blue shortened the stirrup leathers an inch. He collected his shotgun and slicker and stepped on board, barely able to stand the pain he put on his left leg as he heaved himself over. The bay accepted the weight. With luck, Blue thought, he could make the pass in daylight, collect what he needed from the dead animals, and make camp on the other side.

The bay moved smoothly, but Blue wondered how the flatland horse would do in the mountains. Fine, it turned out. The bay moved gracefully up the trail, a calm horse enjoying himself.

Blue made it to the pass at dusk, but there was plenty of light in the west to help him. He switched saddles, putting his own on the bay, and dug into the panniers for the few things he could carry on one animal: a blanket, a slicker, a little parched corn, some lucifers in a cigar tin, the coffee, and a small skillet.

He hung his cartridge belt and holster

around his middle, feeling the weight of the Peacemaker, and set out again, this time working through the thickening dark down the far slope where the killer had lain in wait. He did not look for sign; the killer had gone this way and could go no other because the place was hemmed by the giant shoulders of the mountains. Blue had never been in this country, but knew that the drainage would lead to the Elkhorn River, and that river would flow past Centerville perhaps forty or fifty miles distant.

He let the bay pick its way through timber, and found himself trusting the surefooted animal. Even as dusk turned into pitch-black night, the bay worked cautiously down the drainage. Blue could hear the music of a creek, and once in a while the rustle of a nocturnal animal. The moon rose, and Blue found himself tracing a narrow valley with vaulting rock on one side and brush and gentle slopes on the other.

He halted at an overhang. There was grass for the bay, water, and shelter from the rain he suspected would deluge the mountains before dawn. He could smell the pungence of animals there. He supposed it was close to midnight. There was no reason not to build a fire and boil some of his parched corn, so he set to work.

He often did his best thinking when he was busy at small tasks, and now, as he unloaded the bay and organized his gear, his mind was chewing on the day's events. The killer had chosen not to kill him when he had the chance, and that spoke loudly in Blue's mind. He had yet to fathom what was happening here; whether the killer was luring him along toward some fate, planting a body at his fishing hole and leaving a trail behind with no effort to conceal it, or whether it was all coincidence. Who was stalking whom?

The killer could be ahead, following this drainage, which would take him to the river and Centerville. Or the killer might have quit, urged his horse up towering slopes, and headed in some other direction. Blue would find out in the morning. If the killer was luring him, what was the purpose? If Blue, the hunter, was being hunted, what was the purpose? If the killer intended to ambush him somewhere ahead, but had spared him at the pass, what was the purpose of that?

Hell, there were things beyond a man's ken, and until something else happened, he would just treat it as it was: He was a lawman after a murderer, and one way or another he was going to get his man.

The overhanging ledge projected about five feet over a hollow carved into the limestone by ancient floods, which was fine with Blue. He found ample kindling in the surrounding woods, built a fire downwind of the hollow, boiled some parched corn into mush, spooned the vile stuff down, and rolled into his blanket.

He awakened to a dawn drizzle, as a gust of icy air sprayed rain across his face. The bay stood where he had been picketed, his head low and coppery back black with water. Blue's gear was dry. The shotgun needed to be wiped down. The saddle was safe. He would ride, probably catch up with the killer, who would not expect him in the cold rain. Blue stood stiffly, pulled on damp boots, ate some cold corn mush, donned his slicker, and collected the horse.

That's when his blood ran cold. Tied to the horse's neck was that straw hat with the pink streamers. It lay lightly on the black mane. He had left it at the pass tied to his panniers, which lay beside the dead mule. The straw brim dripped water, and the long ribbons were sodden. But it was the same hat. *And here it was.*

Sometime in that long bleak night, the killer had tied it there. Blue wondered, suddenly, whether he was the hunter or the hunted. He untied the hat, pondering what it meant. It was a familiar hat, somehow. There was something about it that stirred memories, but he could not fathom what they might be. He rotated the hat in his hand, trying to understand the message in it. Maybe there was none. Maybe this stalker was simply amusing himself.

Blue peered into the mist, wondering if some cocky killer was peering at him. There was this about it: The killer was not far off, and Blue figured that might work to his advantage. He led the bay under the overhang, wiped it down, tossed a saddle blanket over it, saddled up, and then rode downslope, feeling the drizzle roll down his slicker and the mist in his face, sliding down his weathered cheeks like tears.

Chapter 6

Blue picked up the trail easily enough. Hoofprints incised the soft earth, and the mist failed to wash them away. They led down the valley, which widened steadily as the creek that carved it tumbled off the mountains and picked up tributaries. At times he rode through lodgepole forest; other times, through verdant parks rife with deer.

He carried the shotgun across his lap but doubted he would use it. Anyone who was more intent on leaving clues than on killing him was unlikely to ambush him. But one never knew. Not that he had much faith in the shotgun just then. This killer was a skilled marksman with a rifle, and if ambush was his intent, Blue would be dead before he knew what hit him.

The bay horse hurried along, happier going downhill than laboring up. The valley widened and leveled, and Blue knew he was not far from the great grassy basins to the west, where cattlemen raised thousands of beeves. The Eastern horse was not obedient, at least not in the Western sense: It wouldn't neck-rein, and he had to saw its head one way or another to steer it. It trembled on slopes. It sidestepped when he tried to mount. But it was a willing and eager animal, and that counted for something. He cursed the death of Hector, and cursed the man who had shot him.

Then, surprisingly, the hoofprints veered to the right, away from the roaring river and straight toward a hogback that hemmed the valley to the north. Blue followed, suddenly more alert. He scrutinized the terrain ahead, finding it dangerous. Talus lay on the steep slope. Copses of aspen and juniper and jack pine dotted the ridge, along with stratified rock; no doubt limestone.

The trail led straight upward, toward a ridgeline a thousand feet above. The killer had urged his horse over shelves of rock, along narrow game trails, over downed logs, ever higher. Blue admired the skills that had guided a horse up a slippery slope without mishap.

Blue reined in his horse, trying hard to remember what lay on the other side of that ridge. Probably another like it, and valleys reaching northwest into the Paraguay, as that stretch of desert on the west edge of the county was called. The killer could head that way and out of the area, out of the territory if he knew how to find the water hole. There was only one in forty miles of parched land, and that so alkaline an animal could hardly stand it. Blue had once chased a gang of stagecoach robbers out there, and caught them when their horses gave out from thirst.

It was raining harder, and the gumbo was treacherous underfoot. Blue ran a hand along the neck of the flatlander bay, under its mane, and decided not to follow the hoofprints that scrambled upward. Half of tracking was simply guessing where the quarry was heading, and Blue suspected that this one was still heading for Centerville and pretending he wasn't.

It was hard to make up his mind. A mistake could cost him his man. But Blue decided to head for Centerville and a visit with Zeke, the town marshal. Among other things, the marshal might be able to identify the bay horse, and Blue would have the name of the victim, and maybe even the name of the killer.

He stared at those fresh hoofprints, the shape so familiar to him now. There was something fishy about this sudden turn right, something that suggested that Blue was being played like a trout by a man skilled at con. He sighed, hoping he wasn't playing the fool.

He could reprovision and get word back to

Barlow, and pick up any news that Barlow had passed along.

Still, he hesitated. He peered upward at that slope, wrestling with a wild itch to race over the top and land on the killer. But that killer was heading for Centerville, and Blue decided to form a little reception committee when the outlaw rode in.

Reluctantly, he abandoned the trail, rode back to the river, and headed through delightful ranch country that was marked by riverside meadows, copses of willows, some jack pine and juniper.

Here was evidence of cattle grazing; the dominion of some stockman over on this west side of the county. Blue rode another five miles before the mist lifted, and two more when he passed into hazy sun. He took off his slicker, tied it behind the cantle, and rode through a thick, moist afternoon. He didn't know how far Centerville was, but if he kept going he should be sleeping in a real bed that night, and he would welcome it.

He spent his time in the saddle mulling things.

Maybe he was making some wrong assumptions. Maybe he was not following the killer but someone who wanted to lead him somewhere or toward some conclusion. He had no way of knowing whether these hoofprints were really those of the murderer of the unknown victim at the fishing hole. Maybe it was even someone trying to give him clues, help him out. Maybe it was all coincidence.

What of that woman's hat? What did it say? Whose hat was it? Was the owner dead? Or was the owner the killer? Or was that hat a message, a threat to some living woman? And why did he keep sensing that the hat was significant to him? It was nothing that Olivia ever wore. Nothing he had ever seen on a mother or aunt or grandmother.

Whoever was escaping from him was also toying with him, and he was very good at it. Maybe this was someone he knew. Maybe someone he had arrested or jailed or caught in times past.

Maybe that trail upslope was intended to decoy him away from something, put him far away from some other crime about to be committed—a crime, like a bank robbery, that he might well stop while on duty in Blankenship.

The more he pondered all this the more Blue fell into bewilderment. He finally decided to go with his intuitions, honed by decades as a lawman, and forget the reasoning and brain beating that led him nowhere. He would meet that son of a gun in Centerville, and it was as plain as that.

He arrived late in Centerville, and had it not been June he would have arrived in darkness. It had been a couple of years since he had ridden into this far southwest corner of the county. The town had shrunk; he could see that. Storefronts were boarded up. The gold and silver miners had ditched it for other El Dorados, and the remaining establishments served the local ranchers and cowboys and their families, a few two-man mines and a few dozen prospectors still combing the canyons and dreaming of bonanzas.

Blue rode past the town marshal's office, a tiny room at the city hall, and headed for the Lady Ann, where he suspected the marshal would be playing poker with his cronies, as he did most every night. Zeke Dombrowski was a bachelor. The saloon was his parlor, and he roomed upstairs.

Blue tied the Eastern horse to the hitchrail, not trusting it to stand untethered, and pushed inside. One overhead light with two lamps burning kept twilight at bay. He saw his man at the table, chewing on a dead black cigar.

"Hullo, Zeke."

The marshal peered up. "You, is it? Half expecting you."

He turned to the rest, four weather-beaten old-timers who constituted the entire patronage of the place this warm evening. "I'm out. Tally me and I'll settle later."

Zeke led Blue toward the door and into the twilight. "Don't want to talk too much around them gossips," he said.

"Expecting me?"

"Yeah, since Barlow sent that picture. I've seen that fellow around here. No way not to see a man dressed in a black suit and boiled shirt like that."

"You have a name?"

"Nope, he just rode in, got himself a nice room at the Aspen, hung around a few days, and vamoosed."

"He must have signed the register."

"He did, but no one can read the signature; big blot on it. Mrs. Grubbe thinks it was something like Horatio Hancock, but she can't remember."

Blue pushed out onto the boardwalk. "That his horse?"

Zeke started. "By damn, it is. Can't miss it, horse like that. Never did see another so copper colored."

"The man's dead. Six bullets did it, and I found his body at my fishing hole."

"No! Dead? That city dude? When was that, Blue?"

"Few days ago." He could hardly count all the damned days.

"Few days ago is when he quit here."

"Alone?"

"How should I know? One day he's here, next day he ain't. I don't go poking around if a man's got lawful business, and this one sure wasn't robbing banks."

"Did he talk to anyone? Anyone meet him?"

Zeke shook his head.

"Any other strangers poking around here?"

"Nope, not as I know of."

"Maybe I'll stay around a few days and find out a few things. You can help me, Zeke. See if anyone knew this man. See if you can come up with a name."

"I'll get right on it, Blue."

"What did you think of the man?"

"Fancy dresser: black suit, cravat, boiled shirt with clean cuffs. Sort of a Philadelphia man. And that horse! So rangy it looks like a running horse to me."

"Thought so, too. Not a likely horse for this country."

"No, it would be too tall for working cows."

"Why would anyone have a horse like this one around here?"

"Good traveling horse, Blue. A get-around kind of horse. Might walk or jog pretty good on flatland."

"It does that," Blue said.

"What are you going to do with it?"

Blue sighed. "Whoever killed the stranger shot my horse and my mule to slow me down. So I'm borrowing this one until I find whose it is. I think the deceased wouldn't mind, seeing as how it's all the transportation I've got."

"Any brand?"

"I've been over it and can't find none," Blue

said. "And with my hands, too, not just eye-balling."

"Eastern horse."

"Western saddle."

"Where's that?"

"It's back on a pass I crossed. This one is mine."

"Nothing there, I suppose."

"Naw. Nothing there, nothing in the man's pockets, either."

"What's that straw hat, Blue?"

"Damned if I know. It was in the field near where the body was. Then the killer got aholt of it and sent me a message with it."

"Message?"

"He got it and tied it to the horse while I sheltered from the rain, and I found it."

"What do you figure the message is?"

Blue sighed. "I have no idea."

"Mind if I see it?"

Blue motioned the marshal forward. The Centerville lawman stepped into the manure next to the rack and plucked up the hat. He untied it, took it into the saloon where he could put some light on it, and ran it around in his fingers a few times. Then he returned to the dark gallery out front.

"Blue, I think I know this here hat. I've seen a gal we both know wearing that thing when she comes in town to shop. It belongs to your daughter."

"Whoa up, Blue. How many miles you come today off the mountains?"

"Forty, maybe more."

"It's near twenty more out to Cooper's place. You figure that's some magic horse?"

"I'll ride light. I know how."

"You better put that flatland horse in the livery barn, get him grained and rubbed, and sit down for a bowl of beans. Then we'll see."

"Got to get out there."

"You're being stubborn. You get yourself a room, grain that horse, and I'll go talk to her. I haven't done a thing all day anyway. I'll take the hat, and if it's hers, I'll warn her, warn Steve, to stay in and stay armed." Zeke paused skeptically. "If that's what you think. Myself, I don't know about this. Might be lots of hats like that. Someone pulls a prank on you just when you're doing something else, and you think it's a threat to your daughter. You got some reason to think it?"

Blue thought it because his gut told him to think it and that was all. "I do," he said.

"Blue, you get some rest, fix that horse a bucket of oats, and first thing in the morning we'll see. I've a notion to take you around town, see who talked to the stranger, maybe find out his name. Get a name on that dead man, get his business, and you're halfway home."

Blue puzzled it. "Zeke, it's not just to warn Tammy. I need some information from her. If she knows who got her hat, or where she left it by accident, and gives me a name, I've got my man figured out."

Zeke sighed, and Blue sensed the marshal was out of arguments. "I guess maybe the livery'll rent you a fresh hoss," he said. "You want company?"

"No, Zeke, information. You find out who that dead man was, whether he got any enemies, all of that. I'll ride."

"You want some beans?"

Blue nodded. He was stiff, and his legs hurt as they always did when a saddle had split them too long. His banged-up knee had been tormenting him all day.

"Well it's too late for Maisie's Place, but they always got a pot of beans in here." Zeke undid the reins of the bay and led him toward the livery barn down at the east end of town.

Blue decided a half hour break wouldn't hurt anything and ordered up some beans from the barkeep.

"Want some eggs too, Sheriff?"

"Sure, and a beer."

Blue was tired. He wanted nothing more than a good bunk and a long sleep, but worry was crawling in his gut, and he knew he wouldn't indulge himself. Not with Tammy in trouble. A killer took her hat. That could mean anything. Tying it to Blue's horse could mean anything from a threat to a prank. But somehow, this was no damned prank.

Zeke returned and slid onto a bench across from Blue. "Hostler knows that horse, but doesn't know the name of the owner. He didn't ask, and the man didn't say. But the man told him that horse is a walker, goes forever at a jig. You ever jig a horse much?"

"I don't know a jig from a jag," Blue muttered.

"Well, it's a gait some of them Eastern nags got."

"You get a name for me tomorrow. And find out if he was with anyone, especially a woman who maybe wore a hat like this. Send what you know to Carl Barlow. I may not be back right away."

"Blue, that's a tough road at night. There's three, four creeks to ford and some slopes."

Blue just shook his head. He was going to his daughter's ranch and that was that. He could only hope he was faster than Trouble.

"Why do you think anyone's after your daughter, Blue?"

"Not my daughter—me. I've got a few enemies. I've put away a few behind bars."

"Revenge?"

Blue broke open the shell of a hard-boiled egg, peeled away the rest of it, and salted the rubbery whiteness. "Anything. I don't know yet. But in all my years of lawing, I've worried about my family. Anyone wants to hurt me, they know how. Anyone wants to get something out of me, they know how."

"Like what?"

"Kidnap my daughter and tell me to release the punk in my jail or she dies."

Zeke nodded. "Me, I ain't so lucky I got to worry about that."

"It's a worry."

The spicy beans, the eggs, and the beer made Blue sleepy.

Zeke saw it. "Blue, you go fetch some sleep. I'll wake you whenever you want."

"Gotta go, Zeke."

Blue stood and dug into his britches for the couple of greenbacks he usually had in his pocket, found some change, and paid.

Zeke walked Blue down the slope to the livery barn. It was full dark and overcast now. "I sure don't know how you're going to make your way," he said.

Blue didn't either, but he was damned if he'd sit still while a killer stalked him. It had come to that. He was being stalked by someone. He'd started out on a manhunt and found himself the hunted.

The barn was dark as ink, but out of the night came a voice.

"Evening, Zeke, Sheriff."

"Fetch the horse, Billy," Zeke said.

"Sure enough."

Blue could scarcely imagine how the hostler knew where to go in that cavern, but he did, and soon enough he emerged in the muddy street, leading the bay horse.

"He et up his oats and some good timothy, too. This here's a fine animal, Sheriff. Don't know how good he is in the mountains, seeing as he's a flatland horse."

"The fellow say where he was from, Billy?"

"New Jersey."

"And what he was doing?"

"No, he didn't say nothing much. 'Take care of the horse; best feed you've got, rub him down.' Like that. He didn't even ask a price. Said he'd be back soon."

"Long way from home. You think of anything he said about his business, you tell Zeke pronto, okay? Think hard!"

"Sure. Now, the oats was four bits and the hay two bits and the stall two bits. I rubbed him, too, and checked his feet."

Blue found a greenback and handed it to the hostler. "That's what I like to hear. You're a good man, Billy."

"You could leave me a tip, Sheriff."

Blue laughed. "Might just," he said, finding a dime. "Buy you a drink, anyway."

Blue checked the saddle in the dim light. His shotgun rested in its sheath, his yellow slicker was rolled up behind the cantle, tied tight with saddle strings. He climbed up and swung a leg over, finding the stirrup with the toe of his boot, and then tied down Tammy's hat, using the pink ribbons.

"Zeke, you mind leading me to the edge of town and starting me on that road?"

"Wish you'd just bunk till dawn, Blue."

But Zeke had taken hold of the bridle and was slowly walking Blue's horse uptown, and then down a mud lane heading south, as far as Blue could tell.

"All right, then, Blue," Zeke said. "You're a man who won't listen to *no* when you've got a *yes* to answer to."

"Bullheaded is what you mean," Blue said.

"That, too."

He started the bay, gave it its head, and let it pick its way in the dark. A horse could do that better than any man could. Funny thing: That tired-out bay acted like he was enjoying the excursion, and started off at a fine clip.

"I guess that's a jig," Blue said aloud. It would eat up the miles, if the bay held out.

A sharp night wind iced out of the mountains and Blue pulled up his collar. He hoped he could sleep. Some cowboys could sleep in the saddle; Blue couldn't, but he could sometimes let himself sink into a loose heaviness, riding like a sack of potatoes. He rode that way for some indeterminate time until the bay stopped. Blue came alert, heard the rush of water, and edged the bay toward a creek. He couldn't tell how deep it was or how wide. He'd been on this trace once or twice and didn't remember any big streams.

"Looks like we're going to wade," he said. "You just go slow now."

The bay stepped carefully, skidding once on slippery river cobbles, and then lunged easily up the far bank. Blue dismounted, let the horse stretch and rest, and then he walked awhile, leading the horse. There was moon enough behind the clouds to give a faint light. But Tammy and Steve's ranch was a long way away, and Blue wished he hadn't been so bullheaded.

That damned killer could read Blue's mind, and that made him testy.

Chapter 8

Blue and dawn arrived at the Cooper ranch at the same time. He rode the tired bay into the yard, admiring the whole lash-up once again. Night mist hugged the green fields. The silvered river oxbowed through the valley, flanked by gentle foothills and blurred black pine forest, while hazy peaks caught the first light. A great quietness enclosed this place.

Steve Cooper's horses stared at Blue from the catch pen. He rode toward the snug, whitewashed ranch house where his daughter lay asleep, along with her little ones and husband. It seemed strange to be the harbinger of danger, bringing worry to this paradise. And yet he must. The battered hat with its pink ribbon dangled from his saddle, urging him on.

He paused before the silent house, seeing no smoke rising from the kitchen chimney. Danger seemed far away. He hesitated. He thought of dismounting and knocking, but chose instead to call through those open sashes, which admitted the gentle night air and brought swift sleep to those within. He saw no smoke rising from the bunkhouse, either, and doubted anyone was in it. Steve and Tammy hired line riders when they needed them at roundup and calving and haying, and got along by themselves the rest of the time. Still, an ancient instinct honed by decades of lawing cautioned him to study a place before making his presence known. He peered into the quickening light, discovering no reason to take alarm.

"Steve! Tammy! It's Blue," he bellowed.

It took a second and third summoning before he spotted Tammy peering out of the upstairs window.

"Dad! What are you doing here?" she cried.

"You could start a pot of coffee while I put up the horse, and I'll tell you."

"That's not Hector. What horse is that?"

"I'll tell that to you, too."

He put the bay into the catch pen, unsaddled it, and rubbed it swiftly. It trotted off to the hay crib and began tearing at the hay there. Blue picked up his saddle and hoisted it onto a rail, and untied Tammy's hat.

Tammy opened the door, and he saw she was wearing a blue wrapper around her skinny frame. A white cotton nightdress peeped through. She was built like her mother. He was glad to see her—very glad. Steve, standing behind her, had stuffed his nightshirt into his trousers.

"Blue! I can't believe it."

"It's a long story," Blue said. "Riding all night."

They gathered around the battered kitchen table, where Blue sank heavily into a chair.

"It'll take a while," Tammy said, stuffing kindling, and then some coal oil to hasten the flame along, into the stove's cold firebox. A whoosh announced the ignition, and Tammy began grinding roasted beans and fetching water.

"This your hat?" he asked, when at last she had started the coffee perking.

She stared, surprised. "Yes, Pa."

"Want to tell me when you lost it?"

"What is this, Blue?" Steve asked. "Why are you here?"

"Lawing," he said. "Been a murder. At my fishing hole, too. And this hat was there, lying in the field."

They stared at him somberly.

He rested his chin on his hand, more tired than he had thought, knowing he owed them an explanation. "It'll take some palavering," he said. "Let me get some coffee into me first. Just tell me about this hat, Tammy."

"We went shopping a few days ago in the spring wagon and I left it in the wagon and it vanished. That's all I know, Dad."

"Centerville?"

"Yes, Centerville. I didn't even notice it until we were on the road back, late afternoon, and I thought the wind had blown it away."

"It was took. And made use of. And maybe you're in danger, maybe not, but I figured to come and tell you."

"Oh, Dad, we're just going along as we always have. If I lost a hat, so what?"

"Well, something's strange, and I haven't got a handle on it yet."

"I guess if you rode all night it's something to worry about," Steve said.

"It is that."

It wasn't until Blue got a half a cup of good Arbuckles coffee into him that he felt up to talking. And then, sipping and talking, he laid out the story that began when he found the stranger.

"That's his horse I rode here. Coppery bay, maybe Thoroughbred, a good flatland walker, anyway. It jigs. Every heard of a horse that does that? Darndest gait I ever sat."

"Tell us about Hector," Steve said.

"Dead. One clean shot through the heart, and almost broke my leg when he went down. My knee still howls."

"How? Where?"

Blue described the encounter at the pass: one moment riding his old horse and leading the mule, the next moment both animals dead and

Blue's leg caught under his horse, and then waiting for the killer to finish him off.

Steve Cooper shook his head.

"What about my hat?" Tammy asked, finally sitting down with her men.

"I first saw it in the field at my fishing hole. I left it at the pass after my animals got shot. Later it got tied around that bay's neck during a rainy night while I slept. How it got there I don't know. Someone's making sport of me, or warning me, or threatening you. Zeke Dombrowski recognized it; I didn't."

"Pa, you wouldn't know one woman's hat from another—not even the one Mom's worn for ten years," Tammy said.

Blue grunted. Sassy girl. "You got to be careful now. I don't know what this is about. But it's your hat, and someone knows it, and that someone's a killer, and there's a message in it somewheres."

"How do you know that?" Steve asked. "How do you know you're following the killer's trail? Maybe the two don't connect at all, Tammy's hat and this murder."

"I've got a hunch is all. You better be careful. Hire some hand you know and trust to help keep guard. If anything happens to anyone here, I'd never forgive myself."

Tammy reached across that old table and pressed her hand on Blue's. "We'll watch out," she said. "And we can fort up here. This house has some loopholes in it, from the early times."

It was still early times as far as Blue was concerned.

"Well, see that you do, dammit," he said. "And watch for the children, too. They're all right?"

"Still sleeping. Sarah needs a lot of sleep."

"Tammy, understand this: There's some out there who'd like to strike at me. Maybe because I wear the star. One way to do it is to threaten my family. A man holding a gun to Olivia's head, man holding a gun to you, man got your kids off somewheres for a ransom or a deal—that's a man that thinks he's got power over me. I've spent a lifetime worrying it, and I'm still worrying it."

She nodded somberly. Blue's coffee was cold, and he stood abruptly, headed for the speckled blue pot on the stove, and poured angrily.

"This is a big country; takes big people to get along in it," he said, wishing he could use better words. "That was Absalom's trouble. Never was big enough."

"Pa—"

He knew he should just shut up. His son disappointed him. Didn't take to anything in the territory—fishing, hunting, ranching, teamstering, not anything at all—and fled to the city and a soft life. An *artist*. Left bitterly too, blaming Blue for everything that went sour in his life, severing his ties with his parents once and for all, or so he said. That was the end of it. Blue never heard from him again. He thought maybe Olivia did, but if so, Blue never heard about it. Once in a while he got a little news filtering in from Denver. The boy had some ability, if sketching stuff counted for something, and he was making his way. But mostly Blue tried to ignore Absalom and bury his disappointment down in the bowels of his mind.

"All right, all right," Blue said, closing off an impending confrontation. Tammy and Olivia were a lot more friendly to the boy than they should be. The hot coffee bit Blue's tongue.

"He's coming here," Tammy said. "To visit me."

"Here? You?"

"I shouldn't have told you. He didn't want me to. We've been writing. He's been planning this for a long time. He's going to spend a month here and paint and sketch . . . and some other things."

"Well, he could have told me."

Tammy shook her heard. "No, he couldn't have told you. There are things you won't hear, especially from him."

The whole business of Absalom put Blue in a bad mood to start with, and his son's secret trip to see his sister filled Blue with brimstone and smoke. Blue was damned if he would tell the boy's mother and have her mooning about the boy for a month.

Blue had wanted to start a family dynasty; lots of sheriffs, fathers and sons, strong men all, honored in the territory. But the boy never took to it and just burrowed his nose into books and sketch pads and neglected his chores. Blue took him fishing, and the boy felt sorry for the fish.

Blue had piled on the chores, too, trying to put some sense into the boy. Cut wood, take care of the horses, prune the lilacs, clean the stove and spread the wood ash for fertilizer, hoe and weed the vegetables, lime the privy, butcher some beef, drive the carriage horse, take the rifle and bring in some meat.

The boy never made meat, and hated to shoot anything, and didn't like to step on an ant. He wouldn't shoot a broken-legged horse to put it out of its misery. He would just set down the rifle and walk away. How the hell did he, Blue, raise a boy like that, anyway?

Things just went from bad to worse, with Absalom recoiling every time Blue told him he needed to make a man out of himself and stop all that soft stuff. It sure wasn't his Smith blood in the boy; who the hell knew about Olivia's Carter blood?

Blue sat there, nursing coffee, remembering. And now the boy was sneaking back to see his sister. Sneaking was the word for it: too cowardly to let his folks know; too scared to face up to his old man.

"Here's what I want you to do," he said. "Tammy, you see any stranger lurking around, you get Steve at once and send word to me. You keep a fowling piece around, full of buckshot, and be ready to use it."

"I still don't know why the hat's so important. It's just a prank," Steve said.

"Some prank. A stranger with no name so far is murdered at my fishing hole and there's that hat, and my horses get shot and the hat keeps showing up."

Tammy stopped her breakfast toil at the stove and turned to her father.

"There is something," she said. "Jack Castle is out. I saw him in town. I'm sure I did."

Jack Castle, Blue thought. At last.

Chapter 9

Blue bolted right out of his chair, spilled coffee, and reached for his revolver.

"Jack Castle. When?"

Tammy stopped stirring the eggs and stared. "A week ago today," she said quietly.

"And you didn't tell me."

Tammy didn't reply; Blue whirled to the windows, studied the serene valley, and then slumped.

"Does Zeke know?"

"You can ask him when you see him," she said. She stirred the scrambled eggs furiously.

"No one told me," Blue said. "The warden didn't say one damned word. Not even a wire to anyone."

"I didn't know either," Steve said. "Should I have known?"

Blue stared unhappily at his son-in-law. The

less he knew about Jack Castle, the better, and Tammy wasn't talking.

"In for eleven years, released after seven," Blue said. "Should have been put away for life." He glared sourly at his daughter. "You pack up and come stay in Blankenship with Olivia," he said. "I'll keep an eye on you. You too, Steve. Get someone to run this place."

"Blue, I don't know what you're talking about," he said.

"Well, it's best you don't."

Steve laughed. "Well, in that case, I'll get to work."

Blue relented. He hated to tell anyone this Smith family stuff, especially since it involved Tammy.

Tammy stood, her skin white and lips compressed, fussing with her wrapper, tucking it under her chin, not liking what was coming.

"Jack Castle is a Blankenship boy gone bad," Blue said. "Tammy was sweet on him."

"Oh, I was not."

"He sure as hell thought so," Blue replied. "Steve, this was before you even came into this country."

"I'm glad of that, I guess. Or should I be?"

"Hell, he didn't go bad; he was always bad," Blue said. "Young, walked like a cat, made the girls smile, big green eyes, always happiest when he was in a little trouble. He had eyes for

Tammy, though. Came sniffing around all the time."

"Pa—"

"We set him down at our table, fed him, got to know him. I didn't much mind him. Hellions are fine with me, long as they stay on the right side of the line. Better than plenty of types of men not big enough for this country." He wished he hadn't said it, but there it was: better than Absalom. Jack Castle had what it took, what the wild land and new country required of a man.

"He was a crack shot, good hunter. Knew what to do if he met a bear, knew how to live outside in bad weather, knew how to deal with two-legged sidewinders, too. Independent. Didn't need parents to mooch from, didn't need government, didn't need handouts. Never knew the meaning of fear.

"He could track anything. Sat a horse with such grace, I don't even know the damned words—like he was riveted into the saddle and was born there, and he has the gift of riding a horse without tiring it out. Some men grind a horse down just by sitting on it, but Jack Castle could take a horse out all day and bring it back as fresh as it started. I was thinking he'd make a fine deputy some day, a fine sheriff too, if Absalom . . ."

"Your eggs are ready," Tammy said, slapping a chipped tan plate before him. It was a wonder the plate didn't shatter.

He didn't care; didn't feel like eating. Didn't feel like anything except putting Jack Castle back behind bars for the rest of his life, and hanging the son of a gun if he killed that stranger.

"Smart, too. He hardly went to the schoolhouse, but he got his letters and arithmetic without half trying, and he could've been a merchant or banker. I watched him do numbers on a slate board, and I thought he could be a bookkeeper or a cardsharp. But he was best at running people, getting them to do what he wanted. I don't know where he got that from.

"His father was dead, a small-time rancher that got pitched off a horse on his head and died when Jack was six or seven. His mother didn't shine none, and was too busy to put a curb bit in Jack's mouth or rein him in. His older brother was a quiet bachelor toiler who put up hay and downed beers each night. But Jack had a way with people, just grinning, calculating, smiling, asking, pushing a little, always toward trouble.

"He liked trouble, like it was the best life offered. Stuffed his nose right into it. Give Jack Castle trouble and he was happy. If he got others into bigger trouble, he was even happier."

"Sweet on Tammy, eh?" Steve grinned at her. "It all comes out."

"Pa, that's enough!" She didn't want Blue to say one more word, and Blue knew why.

All those young years, Jack Castle treated

Tammy as his own property. No one else could dance with her, no one could even talk with her at the barn dances and socials. He'd take her out and they'd disappear into the dark. Blue knew they were spooning, and he found himself watching Castle every moment because one of those times that boy would get into big trouble, or get Tammy into big trouble, and then there'd be hell to pay.

Jack Castle was born dangerous, and that's the type that women fall for the heaviest and hardest. And it was plain that if things went along much further, there'd either be a hasty wedding or Jack Castle would leave the country, and a sweet girl would be ruined. There were plenty of times Blue had stared at his daughter, wondering if that hellion had ruined her. But Tammy had a good head on her, and somehow it didn't happen.

Still, there was something about Jack Castle that Blue liked. He was going to be a *man*, and that's the kind he wanted Tammy to have: a man who could move mountains, give her a fine life and a happy family, and go places in a brand new land rich with promises.

Castle was half like Blue. Settle Jack Castle down some and he'd be just the sort of son that Blue always dreamed of. Blue took him fishing and hunting. They stalked cougars and grizzlies and wolves. Blue showed him every trick there was, until Jack could live in nature as well as

Blue could, and could survive where other and lesser mortals would perish. There wasn't anything Jack Castle did that Blue didn't much mind, at least until things went crazy.

But Olivia saw things differently. She saw the mean jokes Jack pulled, the times he hurt dogs just for fun, the times he humiliated little boys, the times he lifted candy from old Moser's cracker barrels without paying. Blue didn't mind that so much, but Olivia did.

"Blue, you've got to tell him to stay away. He's not right for her," she had said. "There's something in him that's pure trouble."

"Oh, he'll come around. Just needs a little tempering."

"Blue, you're not listening to me," Olivia had said, over and over.

He had been accused of that often enough.

Now Blue sat at Tammy's table, wishing he had listened to Olivia earlier, before things went to hell. Young Castle got wilder and wilder, began "borrowing" horses and returning them just before the owners went to the law. He always seemed to have cash, and learned how to buy hooch out of the back door of saloons like the Indians, and then go up into the hills with his pals and drink it until they were all stupefied. He always stopped short but goaded his young pals into sucking so much booze that they vomited and were sick for days. He enjoyed that, working people like they were cow horses obedient to his rein and spur.

Sometimes word of it got back to the sheriff, and he growled a few warnings at Jack, but those were never enough to stop it. Then one day, when both Jack and Tammy were seventeen, Tammy announced that she was going to hitch up with Jack, and that's when Olivia suddenly became someone Blue had never seen before: a woman as hard as granite.

"The hell you will," she told Tammy, who gaped at the mother who never cussed, leastwise not in front of anybody.

Olivia threw a shawl over her shoulders, marched into the autumnal cold, found Jack hanging out at the livery barn, as usual, and told him never to see Tammy again. If he did, he'd end up in bigger trouble than he'd ever been in before.

Blue went along with it. He knew she was right; it was just that Jack still tickled him, even though he was crossing the line regularly now. Jack was so unlike Absalom that Blue could forgive him anything, even though Blue was the sheriff and Jack was pushing straight into big trouble. It was no longer youthful hijinks; it was something mean and dangerous blooming in that boy.

Jack ignored her and came sniffing around, meeting Tammy behind Blue's back, and that's when Olivia went out one night with the Purdy twelve-gauge shotgun, found Jack, and put a load of buckshot into the livery barn wall three feet to the right of him.

"Next time it's your hide," she snapped, as Jack howled and pulled splinters out of his arm.

Tammy had sulked, but she knew her parents were right. When Jack Castle sneaked around again, she cut him off cold. Blue had to give her credit for that. Even that didn't faze Castle, and a week later he tried to abduct her, employing two stolen horses.

Blue had gotten wind of it, caught the punk, told him to ride: Blankenship was no longer home to Jack Castle. "If I see you in this town again, I'll toss you into my iron cage and let you rot there," Blue had told him.

"How come? What'd I do?"

"You're messing with my daughter, and now you're on the wrong side of the law."

"It's your wife don't like me," Castle had said. "You going to let her rule the roost, old man? You gonna be a skirt-whipped old gelding? You gonna be like Absalom?"

No man had ever talked to Blue like that. "Get out!" he bellowed.

But it hadn't ended. Castle was still roaming the county, getting into worse and worse trouble. Next came some crafty burglaries that Blue knew Castle did but couldn't prove it. Then a rash of cattle rustling, one or two beeves at a time, and then twenty prize shorthorns owned by Emil Bach, the brands altered and the cattle sold a hundred miles south. Blue knew who the hell did it, but Jack Castle was smart, and no evidence led back to him.

Jack Castle was running wild, laughing at Blue, throwing parties back in the mountains, charming the world like some modern Robin Hood, making friends everywhere, still trying to lure Tammy away. And then Blue decided to get the son of a gun once and for all.

A Carter Brothers Stage Company Concord coach was coming from Salt Lake carrying some banknotes for cattlemen's payrolls, and Blue intuited that Jack Castle intended to rob it. Blue knew exactly where. That night he had quietly ridden to the place where the coach slowed and rounded a bend on a narrow mountain road, and he waited there with a pair of double-barreled scatterguns.

Sure enough, Jack and two confederates, all in tan dusters and masks, crawled into hiding a hundred yards away. The coach creaked slowly round the bend, and Castle and his confederates stopped it, jumped the coach, unhitched the six-horse team, disarmed the shotgun rider and passengers, pulled off the money sack, cleaned out the pockets of the passengers . . . and then discovered Blue quietly standing behind them with two barrels of double-ought buckshot, the hammers cocked.

Castle surrendered, grinning, hands waving at the sky.

"Took you long enough, Blue," he said.

The two confederates confessed to seventeen heists, and implicated Jack Castle in them all.

Castle got eleven years. And as he was led out of the county courtroom, he began a little monologue aimed straight at Blue. He swore he would get even if it was the last thing he ever did. He whispered it softly, shook a manacled hand at Blue, and pulled an imaginary trigger.

"Skirt-whipped sheriff," he said as the bailiff hauled him away.

Jack Castle had been a model prisoner. Now and then Blue heard something from other lawmen. Castle was in the pen, doing hard time, smiling, nodding, busting up rock, counting the days.

Tammy soon met Steve, a newcomer in the territory, and married him two years later. Steve was a fine man, a fine son-in-law, a hard-working Westerner who knew cattle and knew how to prosper in a tough business. Their first-born was Joey, and two years later Sarah followed. Blue was pleased with all that: At least one of his children had come out just fine.

So the time has come, Blue thought, worrying about Tammy, Steve, and the two children. *I know who, I know why, but I don't know what's next.*

Chapter 10

Blue woke with a start and sneezed, not knowing where he was. Sunlight filtered through a lace-adorned window. A small face stared at him. A thick red-and-black Hudson's Bay blanket covered Blue. He was lying on a horsehair settee.

Tammy's parlor. The Seth Thomas said four o'clock.

"Joey," he said.

"You slept all day, grampa. Mama wouldn't let me in here."

"What? Didn't mean to," Blue said. He struggled up, stiff and half rested, staring at Tammy's little rascal, who had been waving an iridescent peacock feather on Blue's nose.

"That's why I did it," Joey said.

Blue roared like a grizzly, which sent delightful shivers through Joey.

Last thing Blue knew, he was losing a battle

to stay awake in spite of three cups of coffee. Tammy's warm kitchen and a hot breakfast had done him in.

The revelations of the morning rushed back to him, and he sat up abruptly. His belt and holster hung from a cowhide chair. Everything seemed peaceful.

"Where's your ma?"

"Henhouse."

"Why aren't you getting the eggs?"

"Girl stuff," Joey said. "Sarah can do that."

"Chores are everyone's business, and the sooner you get them done, the more time you have."

Blue was full of lectures. The younger generation was going to hell, and he was going to do whatever he could about it.

He stood and stretched, actually grateful that Joey had tickled him with the peacock feather. A killer was on the loose, and his family was endangered.

"She take a gun?" he asked.

"An egg basket." Joey stared at him. "She gonna shoot the hens?"

"Well there's a rooster or two that deserves it," Blue said.

Blue tried out his legs and found they supported him fairly well; not at all badly after all those years. His knee still hurt. He found a coffee pot with some lukewarm java in it, as black as spades. The stuff curdled his gizzard, but he downed a cup, all the while peering outside at those slumbering, sunbaked slopes and endless fields and grazing red shorthorn cattle and drifting puffs of clouds.

"Where's your pa?" he asked Joey.

"Making fence."

Blue felt his old worries crabbing through him, and headed out into the sunny yard. He could get back to Centerville by late evening, talk with Zeke, make some plans. He didn't even know where the hell to start. The trail was colder than the north pole. Somewhere out there, Jack Castle was roaming like a rabid wolf, fueled by hatred.

Blue walked out to the catch pen to saddle up the bay horse. He opened the gate, looked over the stock, mostly ranch animals, and didn't see the bay. He headed for the barn. Steve must have stalled it, probably wanted to grain it. Blue entered the cavernous red-washed building and was smacked with the pungence of fresh hay and the acrid smell of old manure. A swift survey revealed nothing but empty stalls. Where the hell had Steve Cooper put that horse?

Blue stormed out of the barn, and found Tammy rounding a corner carrying a basket. Little Sarah was tagging along.

"You're up," she said.

"Where the hell did Steve put that bay?"

She smiled wryly at his grouchy greeting.

"Here, love, take these to the kitchen," she said, handing the basket to Sarah. "And be gentle."

"Hi, Grampa."

"Don't you break none of those eggs."

Sarah stared at him, and then wheeled away.

"Steve didn't touch your horse," Tammy said, heading for the catch pen. "He rode Glory and had a mule packing some wire."

Blue watched her stride toward the pen, the breezes whipping her brown dress around her thin frame. She was a woman any man could be proud of.

She stared. "It was here this morning," she said, her face taut.

"You got any paddocks?"

"Yes . . . this." She waved at a pole-fenced pasture that was empty of all animals.

"Dammit, that horse is somewhere," Blue said. "You got any holes in your fence?"

That got him a glare from her. This was the best-kept ranch in the county, and Steve meant to keep it that way.

He stormed back to the catch pen, worry building in him like a summer storm. "I'll need to saddle up a nag and go looking for that bay. Must've got out."

"That buckskin's coming along," she said. "Steve's been working him. Just needs watching. He hasn't been under saddle long."

"Okay, okay."

Blue headed for his saddle, which hung over

a corral rail, and that's when he saw it. His scattergun was gone. The sheath was empty.

"What the hell?" he said. "Tammy, did Steve borrow my scattergun?"

She stared mutely at him, fear building in her eyes.

"Of course he didn't," he said. "Get into the house, and don't walk; run. Don't let anyone in."

She fled, and he watched her race toward the porch. Out of ancient instinct he slid his six-gun out of its nest at his hip, but there was nothing there, nothing to shoot at. He squinted at the distant lines of trees, the empty green meadows, the circling crows, the meandering and sparkling creek, the roofs of buildings, the occasional black stump that dotted the slopes. He was holding a useless damned piece of iron in his fist.

Nothing. A worm of fear crawled along his gut. *Castle here.* Another calling card or two. What was all this? The man was stalking Blue Smith and his family. How'd he know to come here? Had he trailed Blue through the night? Did Zeke tell him? What the hell?

Blue slid into the catch pen with a lariat and eased through the horses. The buckskin was leery and had a knack for putting itself behind half a dozen other nags. Blue was getting impatient. He hadn't had a good horse since Hector was shot.

But quick and catlike, Blue tossed his loop and it settled over the young ranch horse. The buckskin didn't fight, which surprised him. Steve had gotten a good start on him. The horse had a gentle eye, but it shivered when Blue ran a hand along its back. Well, it would do.

He bridled and saddled the buckskin, worrying about what to do. He didn't want to leave Tammy unguarded. He wanted to find the bay. He wanted to talk to Steve. He couldn't go after Castle until he knew that Steve was back at the ranch house and looking after Tammy and the children.

Tammy stood on the porch watching, her children gathered at her skirts.

Blue boarded the buckskin and found it obedient. "Where's Steve?" he asked.

She pointed toward Axe Canyon, a steep defile that led to the hills and into a hidden, mountain-girt meadow.

"He's making fence," she called.

"I'm going to get him. You get yourself inside and pull the shutters and bar the door."

"Oh, Pa . . ."

"Do it!"

She herded the children inside, and he watched the door swing shut and heard the bar fall. It seemed absurd, forting up on this peaceful June afternoon, with the whole world glistening sweetly, the zephyrs gliding through the waving grasses, and the cattle resting content and fat.

But fear crabbed at Blue. *Jack Castle.*

The buckskin had a rough trot that hammered Blue's tailbone, so he contented himself with a fast walk. That was good. He could keep an eye on the dark patches of trees where trouble might lurk. He didn't know what the hell he would do armed only with a six-gun if he ran into Castle, but he would play the hand he was dealt. For half an hour he rode through the lazy afternoon, piercing a narrow hemmed by ancient gray limestone, following a narrow path that showed recent use, with horse and mule prints melding together.

Then at last he burst into the hidden valley, a paradise of sloping green meadows guarded by vast slopes that vaulted into timber and high crags. He wondered why Steve was building fence in such a naturally enclosed pasture, but ahead he spotted Steve's project, a paddock to hold cattle for branding or castrating or doctoring.

Steve's horse and mule stood beside a runnel, picketed on good grass. There was a line of newly set posts gleaming whitely. But Steve was nowhere in sight. Uneasily, Blue pushed the buckskin the last two hundred yards. Steve had to be around there somewhere.

"Steve?"

Blue rode ahead, his belly crawling with

worry, seeing no sign of Steve Cooper. He reached the tethered horse and mule, noted the rolls of barbed wire, the spade, the auger, and the pick. But not Steve.

Blue dismounted uneasily and tied his horse to a post.

"Steve?" he yelled.

Maybe Cooper had headed into the thickets nearby.

"Steve?"

Then he saw Steve, lying in tall grass, face up, staring sightlessly at the sky, his shirt and britches soaked with blood.

The sight punched Blue backward. He couldn't breathe.

Steve Cooper dead. Tammy . . . Tammy . . . Steve . . .

Blue hung on to a fence post.

Oh, Tammy . . . How could he say to her what he had to say?

Chapter 11

Blue had trouble making his legs move, but at last he stood over Tammy's husband.

Buckshot, Blue thought, probably from his own scattergun, at close range. None had touched Steve's face. Steve stared innocently at the sky. Dead at twenty-nine, murdered for nothing more than loving and marrying Tammy, the daughter of the sheriff. Blue watched the green-bellied flies swarm upon the bloodred shirt.

Blue didn't know how to tell Tammy. It was beyond him, breaking this news, showing her this.

He studied the silent slopes, the wind-danced grass, the circling of a hawk.

"All right, Jack, I'm coming. I'll get you," he said, hoping the breezes would carry his message across the fields, over the mountaintops, down the rivers.

He half expected a bullet to sear through him, but it didn't, and he knew that Castle would play this out his own way, tormenting Blue as much as possible first. Castle's old curse came to mind, and with it the shape of Castle's revenge.

Blue did what he had to do. He untied Steve's ranch horse and set the mule free. It would trail along behind.

Then he knelt over Steve, turned him over, and found that the buckshot had blown clean through his son-in-law. Out of old habit, Blue turned Steve's pockets out, finding nothing but a jackknife.

Then he gently slid his arms under the body and struggled to his feet. Steve weighed plenty. Steve's horse jerked back, wild-eyed. Blue let the horse sniff, but that didn't calm the animal. It took two more tries to get Steve's body draped over Steve's saddle and tied in place. And by the time Blue had finished, he was soaked in Steve's blood. It was fitting. Steve's wounds were his own wounds. Steve's blood was his own blood.

Blue started back to the ranch house in the summer afternoon's long light, leading Steve's horse behind the buckskin and trying to find words to say to Tammy. He had no words. Angry clouds were building; it would rain this night of tears.

It seemed longer going back than riding out.

Or maybe he was just going slower, delaying the bad moments to come. But in time he debouched from Axe Canyon and rode slowly across the fields, the low light throwing long, hard shadows.

He stopped before the ranch house, not knowing whether he could do this thing. And yet he had to.

He rode in slowly, and Tammy saw him from the doorway and ran toward him—ran screaming, a wail that chilled his marrow, and then she reached him and took it all in.

"I knew it, I knew it, I knew it, I knew it," she cried.

"Castle."

"Oh, Steve!"

She plunged toward Steve's nervous horse. It shied. She stopped suddenly, gaping at the blood.

"Oh, oh, oh," she groaned, and then found Steve's limp hand and held it beside the horse.

Blue dismounted and threw an arm around her shoulder, knowing he had no comfort to offer. She was shaking. He wished to God he could console her but there were no words. He'd been a sheriff a long time, and had been in the middle of hell more than once, but never with his own.

Blue studied the ranch porch, not seeing the children and glad of it. He didn't want them to see this.

"Tammy," he said gently, "keep the children away."

"I knew it, I knew it," she said.

He led the horses toward the barn in the long golden light. Somehow he had to deal with all this.

"Tammy, there's Joey on the porch."

Tammy let go of that limp hand and staggered back to the ranch house. "No, Joey, you stay there," she cried.

Blue watched her herd the child inside, and continued on into the big dark barn. Once in that concealing shadow, he untied Steve, lifted him off the horse, and set him on some straw bedding. Steve was as heavy a burden as Blue could carry.

He made himself unsaddle the horses and turn them into the catch pen. The mule trotted in, as well, and headed for the hayrick.

Blue found a keg and sat on it. It all depended on him now. Keep her safe. Comfort her and the children. Figure this out. He thought of his fishing hole and the cutthroats lurking in that quiet pool, and his line sailing over them and dropping his fly upon them in the sweet quiet. He thought of Tammy, bereaved, her husband dead because Blue wore the badge and had to deal with bad men.

He rose wearily, found a horse blanket, and covered Steve.

She returned after a time, he didn't know how long, slipping into the dusky barn.

"They're in bed," she said. She stared at the old blanket and the still form under it, and then slumped down beside Steve's body. She touched the horse blanket. Found Steve's cold hand and took it. Closed her eyes.

The barn was very quiet.

Blue settled down beside her and took her other hand, and they sat beside Steve Cooper for a long time. For the moment, Tammy was holding up. The grief would flow later.

"We'll go to Centerville in the morning. We'll need your spring wagon," he said.

"I haven't told the children."

Blue nodded. That was her province. She would decide where and when.

"You know someone who can look after the place?"

"Not nearby."

"We'll have to put the animals out on pasture."

"There's the chickens, and the dogs . . ."

"I'll find someone for you, Tammy. Zeke will know of someone."

She didn't reply. She wasn't crying, but he knew she would, away from him, alone. The Smiths held everything in. He had taught them to. Never let the world see anything. Maybe that was wrong. He hated tears, but now he wished she would weep.

"Tammy, maybe you should be with the little ones," he said. "I'll be along."

She rose wordlessly and vanished into the darkness. He had one or two things to do. He found a candle lantern in the tack room, lit it with a lucifer, and hunted for a tarpaulin and some rope. He settled for an ancient blanket, rolled Steve into it, and lashed the bundle with thong. Then he tugged the spring wagon into the barn and lifted Steve into the back of it. That would have to do.

He found his way to the house mostly by instinct because clouds obscured the stars, and settled in a rocker on the porch, his revolver in hand. He heard no noise within. The crickets were chirping.

Steve had died. Who else would? How did the stranger fit in, the one at the fishing hole? Why Steve? Was it simply because Steve was the husband of the woman Castle wanted and could not have? Murdered for nothing more than that, but nothing less? It seemed likely.

Or maybe it was all Castle's plan to torture Blue by destroying his family one by one. Was that it? Maybe Tammy would be next, and then Blue himself. That was the only sense he could make of it. Castle would torment Blue as much as possible, and Blue would be the last to die, filled with grief. Jack Castle was fully capable of thinking like that.

Blue grunted. Jack Castle wouldn't get that

far. A man whose criminal design was obvious was a man who could be trapped and brought to justice. But Jack Castle was no ordinary man. Blue had never known a man so able, so audacious, so strong, so devoid of conscience. He had planned this whole thing for seven years, engrossed Blue in a scenario that began with a stranger's murder. It was as if Castle was a puppeteer, and Blue was dancing on his strings. Castle had that gift; he was always one jump ahead of everyone else.

Whatever happened next, it would be the unexpected, and it would be designed to hurt Blue as much as possible.

Blue's mind worked feverishly. Get Tammy and the children to Centerville and some safety. That seemed the first and most important thing. Then go after Castle, go after him doggedly. Blue knew he was a plodder, not nimble like Castle, but Blue could hang on, sink in his bulldog teeth, and maybe Castle would make his mistake. The bright, swift ones usually did.

Blue slept little that night. He stayed in the rocker on the roofed porch, even when a soft mountain drizzle enveloped the ranch. He stayed in that battered chair, his revolver in hand, barring the door. Dawn arrived gray and cold and dripping, and Blue's old bones ached from the chill.

But Tammy was safe. That was all he could give her, some safety, and too little of that.

In the gloomy dawn Blue threw the harness on Steve's dray horse, buckled it up, and hooked the dray to the spring wagon, all before he heard any stirring from the house.

Tammy met him at the door.

"I've told them," she said.

He entered, found them eating silently—sliced bread and preserves—and helped himself to some bread. It was a cold meal.

Blue headed out, turned the livestock loose, opened the door of the henhouse, and set out scraps for the dogs.

Tammy herded the children to the wagon.

"Is that Daddy?" Joey asked, examining the bundle.

She nodded, settled into the seat, and collected the lines.

Blue rode Steve's ranch horse.

So they abandoned paradise, which is how the Smiths had seen that ranch, and rode slowly for Centerville. Blue was alert and restless, knowing what a poor defense he could throw up against a man armed with a rifle and a shotgun. Somewhere, Castle would be watching. Maybe he would even be amused to see Blue doing exactly what he had to do: getting Tammy to safety.

But nothing happened. Blue figured nothing would. Castle would take his time. They reached Centerville late in the morning. So mournful was their passage down Center Street that people paused, stared, tried to fathom what lay within that blanketed bundle. At Maisie's Place, Blue halted, looking for Zeke, who emerged into the wan sunlight, studied the wagon, and motioned them toward the town hall and the marshal's office.

"He's dead, Zeke. Castle got him."

"Dead? Steve Cooper?"

"Castle was just waiting his chance."

"What for, Blue?"

"Ask Castle."

"Because I'm a Smith, and because he was my husband," Tammy said.

Zeke absorbed that. Blue said, "She needs guarding, Zeke."

"She needs a lot more than that, Blue. I'll look after her."

Blue left her there and took Steve to the cabinetmaker, because there was no undertaker in Centerville.

"I want a box—a good box, a proper damned box," he said.

"For Steve Cooper, sir, the best wood on my shelves: mahogany."

"Make it better than that," Blue said. "Make it oak or walnut."

An hour later, with Tammy safe in town and the marshal looking after her, Blue started back to the ranch. Somewhere in that moist soil there would be a trail, and he would follow that trail to the end of the earth if he had to.

Chapter 12

Blue rode all the way out to the ranch again that bitter day, wearing out Steve Cooper's horse. But there were others, and he had Tammy's permission to outfit himself. He sat on the horse half asleep as it plodded wearily home, needing no direction.

Jack Castle wouldn't expect Blue to start after him. Not yet. Not until after the funeral, not until after the grief. And that would be Castle's first mistake.

The Centerville marshal had swung into action, settled Tammy and her two children in the Hjortsberg Hotel, and set up a twenty-four-hour guard. Zeke said he would send a man out to the ranch to look after the stock and the dogs. He would post a two-hundred-dollar reward for Castle, get it printed up by the Centerville *Weekly Clarion,* and nail it to every damned fence post in the county.

The Coopers were well-liked people in Centerville, and Blue knew there would be help and comfort for Tammy. He felt bad about leaving her alone, especially during the funeral, but he did what he had to do, and that was what made him a lawman. He did the hard things, and his family knew it.

He had to trust Zeke Dombrowski to look after her. Zeke spent most of his days playing poker, but what else was there for a town marshal to do in Centerville? Zeke was a good constable. One time he'd stopped a bank robbery and sent the whole lot manacled together for trial in Blankenship. Now he would spring into action.

Blue had taken a moment to write Olivia a letter; it would reach Blankenship before he got back. He scraped out the words with a post office pen—hard words wrought from lumpy post office ink, angular letters dug into paper—and then he blotted his writing and paid the two cents to the postal clerk through a wicket in the hardware store.

Olivia would have someone, maybe Carl Barlow, read the letter to her, and she would learn that the man Blue was after was Jack Castle, who had sat at her kitchen table many a time. Learn that her son-in-law had been shot dead and Tammy was in Centerville under guard. Hard news, scraped onto paper, read to her by someone who could see.

Blue felt bad about it. She had been a sheriff's wife for as long as he could remember, and she was tougher than he was. But this news would stagger her. He held back one bit of information: that their son, Absalom, was intending to visit Tammy and Steve and had kept the visit a secret from his parents.

Now Blue was riding, now he was lawing again, tracking an outlaw. Now he was the hunter, not the hunted, and he liked that. As he rode he chewed on the case, nipped at ideas, and tried out theories like beaver-felt hats, but nothing quite fit.

So he would do what lawmen do: plod along, hunting, looking, waiting for the break. And that break might come soon, because Castle would be lounging around out there, not running, and that's where that killer had underestimated Blue.

The ranch lay somnolent in that peaceful time of day just before sundown. Blue paused, sharp-eyed, and studied the place, seeing nothing amiss. The horses grazed or stood motionless. Cattle dotted distant slopes. The low sun sinking in the northwest lit the eastern crags, tinting the high snowpack gold. The ranch buildings lay in lavender velvet. How much Steve and Tammy had loved this place. Blue loved it too.

Blue unsaddled and turned Steve's horse into the catch pen. Not a bad mare. He'd done nothing but ride dead men's horses for days. He missed Hector, a horse who knew what Blue was going to do before Blue did.

Wearily, he trudged to the dark ranch house, once the abode of fresh-baked bread, children's laughter, dreams, struggle, achievement, and hearty hospitality. Even so, caution did not desert Blue, and he studied the windows, the darkened veranda, the surrounding shrubs, looking for the glint of steel. But he saw nothing.

The porch echoed hollowly underfoot, and Blue pushed the creaking door open, swung to one side out of the door light, and waited. Only silence met him. He decided not to ignite a lamp; not to give away his presence. He planned to spend the night; he couldn't do anything until morning, and then he would ride out of Axe Canyon and pick up the trail.

Blue headed for the hearth, wanting Steve's rifle, an old Springfield rifled musket, a relic of the Civil War, the only weapon Steve kept on the place. It would do. Blue had shot identical rifles during that war, knew how to load the waxed cartridges, cap the nipple, and shoot. Not very fast, those heavy old Springfields, but they had an advantage over the Henry or Winchester repeaters the cowboys were toting these days: range. And accuracy, too. Maybe one of those old cartridges would have Jack Castle's name on it.

But it would be a long and heavy piece of iron to haul in a saddle sheath.

Blue filled a pocket of his canvas duck coat with cartridges and a small box of caps, and then ransacked the kitchen for grub. He was hungry, but first he wanted to put together a kit. A manhunt required some planning. He'd heard of a dozen sheriffs who'd raced off, hot on the heels of their quarry, only to be driven home again by hunger or cold or the want of bullets or some fool thing that a few moments of planning would have eliminated. He ransacked the pantry for corn, beans, and whatever might be handy on the trail.

Two loaves of bread dough sat in their tin pans. They had risen and were awaiting the oven. But he would not bake them. He wolfed down the last of Tammy's bread and pried open a can of stewed tomatoes and downed that. In the springhouse he found some milk and eggs, but decided not to cook the eggs; that would make smoke. He shook the milk can until the cream was well blended, poured a glass of it, and sipped.

In the last light of a hard day, he slid out to the pasture and slowly herded the horses toward the catch pen. When they were in, he latched the gate and studied the night-hazed slopes, still alert for trouble, and then ghosted his way back to the dark ranch house. He would sleep if he could.

Steve's nondescript dogs crowded onto the porch, tails wagging, wanting to be fed, so Blue hunted for some scraps, found nothing, and settled for some beef hanging in the springhouse.

"There'll be someone coming to care for you fellows," he said, pitching a piece of beef to each of the three mutts.

But he wondered what would come of this place.

Sleep caught him swiftly; he had driven himself as far as a man could, and he knew nothing until the dawn light awakened him. The house lay silent, and he wondered why he felt the imminence of trouble.

He was feeling rested but sore. He wasn't used to so much time on horseback, his legs split so wide apart. This day he would start hunting and he wouldn't stop hunting until he had his man.

He scraped the stubble off his cheeks, using cold water because no hot was in the stove reservoir. He dressed and stepped into the gray hush of the valley, the Springfield in hand.

Blue stopped cold.

A black dog hung by its heels from a cord tied to the porch roof. It had been gutted. Its tongue lolled out of its mouth, which was curled back in the rictus of death. Steve's favorite dog, the one he called Muttonhead.

So Jack Castle was still keeping an eye on him. Toying with him. Mocking him. Blue studied the ranch yard, looking for more trouble, but did not find it.

It had taken great skill to do that: kill a dog and keep the others from barking in the night, while Blue slept. Jack Castle had gifts beyond imagining. But he was showing off, and that could be his mistake. There would be fresh tracks inviting Blue to follow.

But Blue decided he wouldn't follow. That was a funny thing. He was tired of being led by the nose by a clever killer trying to torment him. Now Castle wanted him to find those tracks and follow toward some other little surprise, but Blue was damned if he would, stubborn as he was.

He knew what he would do: He would ride up Axe Canyon and find the older tracks there, the tracks of the man who rode down Steve Cooper and murdered him with a shotgun—tracks Jack Castle might not want him to follow, that would lead into the high country and maybe even into Castle's hideaway.

Blue stepped out of the shadow of the porch, crossed the yard, studied the horses in the catch pen and realized that Castle had left them alone, almost as if he were inviting Blue to saddle up and follow. Blue's old stock saddle rested on the corral rail, unmolested.

Maybe Castle was watching him right then from one of those vast slopes; maybe not. Maybe he had a fancy brass spyglass. Maybe

Castle was watching Blue through buck-horn gun sights. Blue didn't care.

He bridled and saddled Steve's ranch horse, then haltered, saddled, and loaded the buckskin he had ridden two days before and put the rest of the stock out to pasture. He steered toward Axe Canyon, leading the burdened buckskin, climbing slowly along a laughing creek. Then, just before the canyon enclosed him, he paused and twisted around in the saddle.

Below him was Steve and Tammy's paradise, dew glistening on the grass, the snowcapped ridges orange in the first light. He felt a moment of tenderness, and then sorrow. So much lost. Then he touched his heels to the flanks of the horse.

"All right, Jack Castle, I'm coming," he said. "You'll think I'm behind you, where you want me, until you find out I'm in front."

insight into the killer's mind. Blue was betting the jackpot that Castle wasn't ready to ambush him; Castle was enacting a dream he had nursed during all those years in the pen to torment Blue as much as possible and then kill him later. Yes, Castle would enjoy that, like a cat toying with the field mouse it would soon kill.

So Blue rode ahead fatalistically. If a bullet felled him, then he was wrong. It was as dark and bleak as that. The thin trail traced a noisy creek that stair-stepped down the mountain, pouring icy water onto Cooper's meadows far below. Sometimes he pierced through thickets of pine, inhaling air balsamic and pungent, while other times he circled around rockslides, where marmots studied him or dodged, and the morning sun lit up pockets of yellow blooms.

Any of those shifting landscapes could have harbored a killer, but Blue knew they wouldn't. By midmorning Blue topped what he thought was a pass, but found himself instead on a hanging plateau surrounded by snow and rock. The world below him spread out, blue and breathtaking. He could even see Centerville, but Blankenship lay beyond his vision to the northeast. From this amazing aerie, with a big enough telescope Castle could have seen everything of consequence in thirty miles.

Blue paused to rest his nags, and slid off Steve's horse. It was time to ride the buckskin for a while. But there was still one thing to do:

He walked back to the edge of the plateau, which afforded a view down Axe Canyon, and studied his back trail for several minutes. Satisfied that no one was behind him, he pulled the saddle off the tired ranch horse and threw it over the jittery buckskin. A fool green-broke horse in the mountains was a dangerous thing, and Blue knew he would need to be careful. But Blue was always careful around horses.

Castle had used this high country meadow for the same things: switching horses, rest, and observation. Blue found hoofprints and also boot prints; the familiar, wide boot prints he first spotted clear back at the fishing hole. They were a killer's boots, and the shape of their print had been scorched deep into Blue's mind. In a way, that pleased him. He had followed those boots from there to here; sixty or seventy miles as the crow flies. He knew who he was pursuing and he had a motive, and now his task was not to dog Castle like a bloodhound but to outguess him.

A biting wind swept the high plateau, the air straight off the snowfields above. Blue ignored the chill and began circling the plateau, finding plenty of tracks, many of them jumbled. But what counted were those that left this crow's nest for the low country. He spotted none that led upslope into the forbidding gray and snowy peaks high above timber; the ones that interested him led downhill. One trail dropped toward the Cooper range, but not via Axe Canyon. Another went he knew not where, but a trail on the far northern edge of the plateau plummeted steeply toward Centerville.

And that's where he found the hat. There it was. Tammy's hat, the one with the pink ribbon, tied to a bristlecone pine, flapping in the wind, waiting for Blue. Stolen right out of Tammy's house when Blue was taking Tammy to Centerville. Blue blinked, not believing his eyes. Then he rode to it and raged at it, raged at the killer who was toying with him as if he were an idiot, the killer who made the fool out of him and laughed all the while.

Blue quieted himself, stepped off the buckskin, untied Tammy's hat, let the buckskin sniff it, and anchored it to the pommel with a saddle string. The killer wanted him to rush for Centerville to protect Tammy. Jack Castle was jerking the puppet strings again.

Blue quieted himself. He might or might not head for Centerville on this trail. His task was to outthink Castle, and he was doing a poor job of it. It was as if Castle had been reading Blue's mind, absorbing Blue's ways, from boyhood, and knew how the older man would react. The truth of it was that Castle was uncanny.

He hated to admit it, but he was no closer to finding Castle than he had ever been. And Castle was roaming mighty big country; hundreds of square miles. He might even be far away, out of the whole territory by now. He might have a confederate planting these warnings, leading Blue around as if he were a bull with a ring in his nose, while Castle rode away to California or some place like that.

Tracking was a lonely business. Blue sat his horse there, feeling as if he was the only person left in the world; as if all those good people down in Blankenship and Centerville didn't know their sheriff was up in the high lonely, with only the soughing wind for a friend, hunting a vicious man who had once almost been a son.

Blue steered the buckskin off the bleak plateau and rode quietly for two or three miles into deepening timber, where the air was still and the forest floor was covered with brown pine needles. This was a dry trail, except for springs every little while that leaked their waters into grassy bogs.

At one of these little parks he stopped, hoping the mosquitoes wouldn't be bad, and set up camp for the night. The forest guarded the glade so completely that Blue could barely glimpse the twilit sky, but that was good. He could have a fire that would not be seen.

An odd loneliness pervaded this place and his mind. He cussed his own pride; he should have gotten together a large posse, divided it into platoons, and sent fifty men into the mountains to hunt down Jack Castle. But he was too proud to rely on others; it was like using crutches, and he was damned if he would send large gangs out only to return empty-handed.

Blue collected some downed wood, dry on top but moist on the bottom, broke it up, added tinder, and started a fire with a little gunpowder from one of his Springfield cartridges and a lucifer. After a long, sullen moment the flame took, and soon Blue had some parched corn boiling in the skillet. Miserable fare, but it kept him going. He didn't need much; never did, not even someone to talk to.

He ate the mush with a flat spatula he whittled, there being no spoon, and began making a bed, scraping sticks and pebbles away before he laid out his bedroll. The horses grazed peacefully on their picket lines. Blue was feeling old. Maybe Castle was the better man and letting Blue know it, but that didn't matter: Better men made mistakes. And Blue's job was to catch Castle, not engage in some duel.

Dammit, he would have to get a posse together, and he hated the very idea. He hated all of this, especially that Jack Castle was waltzing around him as if he were some punch-drunk boxer stabbing slowly at wherever Castle had been moments before.

But Blue wasn't going to stop.

"I'm coming, Castle," he said.

In the morning he started along that trail north, and soon found himself in an alpine paradise, where dark Steller's jays and tuxedo-colored magpies set up a ruckus as he rode through verdant parks and meadows and aspen groves and stands of spruce. Why was nature so promiscuously beautiful just when his heart hurt?

He switched horses halfway down, knowing that descending was harder on a burdened horse than ascending. The trail led along a laughing creek that seduced his wariness until he knew he was as vulnerable as a greenhorn.

Then, toward the supper hour, he found himself on a shelf of land overlooking Centerville, which basked in the June sun. A half hour later he hitched his horses at the Hjortsberg Hotel, stepped painfully into the gummy street, feeling the long day's ride in his bones, and entered.

The place was not guarded. He lumbered down a long corridor to number 6, and rapped.

She opened at once.

"Pa!"

"Is everything all right?"

"Yes. . . . I mean, I'm safe."

"There's no guard."

"Zeke doesn't have the men. And I can take care of myself."

She motioned him in. The room was cramped, with a spare cot. The children leapt up and crowded about their grandfather. He patted them.

"I don't like it here," Joey said. "Can we go out?"

"Soon, son," he said.

"What about you? Did you find him?" she asked.

He shook his head, hating to admit defeat. "He left a few calling cards, Tammy. He killed Steve's black dog and hung it from the porch . . . while I slept."

"Oh, oh . . ."

"Muttonhead, Muttonhead," Joey wailed. The boy dove for the cot and buried his head under a blanket.

"Tell me how it went, Tammy. . . . If you want to."

He pulled his hat off his head, and finding no place to sit, settled gingerly on the edge of the bed, hollowing the chenille spread, as out of place in this tiny enclave as a bull.

"You mean Steve." She stood at the window, which opened on an alley, her almond eyes staring into the hills. "We buried him yesterday. Just about everyone in town came. Zeke even had some guards posted around, just in case."

"Was it a good service?"

"Oh, Dad, he's gone, and it didn't matter what they said. I don't remember a word. He's gone."

She had found no comfort, then. He studied her, finding her drawn and gaunt and dark eyed, the pain radiating from her thin face.

"I'll go to the cemetery and pay my respects," he said miserably.

"Dad, we're going back to the ranch. I can't stand it another hour here."

"It's not safe."

"Then I'll go and bear the risk. That's my home, that's where I belong, that's where my children can heal. Not here. You can come with us tomorrow or not, but we're going."

Blue thought of that hat still tied to his saddle, its pink ribbons trailing down the side of the horse.

"Zeke have someone out there yet?"

"Yes, a man called Cletus. Zeke says he's reliable. Zeke's even deputized him a few times. I know who he is. He's a drover, too."

"Well," Blue said, "you have to play the cards you're dealt. But Jack Castle's not done with you."

She straightened, her gaze unwavering, her resolve deepening before his eyes. "You taught me to take care of myself," she said. "And I will."

He nodded. That was her true inheritance. He had no money to bequeath to her, but he had a vision of what it took to live and prosper in a new land, and that he had given her—and tried to give to Absalom.

"Supper's on me," he said. "Maisie's Place open?"

"Oh, boy, outa here!" Joey said.

They paused at the hotel door, and Blue studied the empty business district. They were all living with fear now, hardly taking a step without surveying empty windows and dark alleys.

He led them across the street toward the café, his mind awhirl. He couldn't stop her from going back to the ranch, but maybe there was some good in it. Castle would know it soon enough and come prowling. Maybe Blue could set a trap.

Chapter 14

Blue found Zeke at his usual post at the green poker table, a fat stack of white chips before him and a yellow cigar slimed into a corner of his purple mouth.

"Blue," Zeke said. "Let me fold." He quit the hand and swiftly cashed in.

Moments later the town constable and Blue strolled up the dark artery of Centerville, lit only by the eerie solstice twilight that turned the mountains into black teeth. The tang of wood smoke hung in the air, the residue of evening cooking fires. Blue absorbed the peacefulness of the place. Crime just didn't visit Centerville anymore, not since the mining died away.

"I had a man full-time at the hotel lobby until after the funeral," Zeke said. "Hardly seems necessary anymore, and I had trouble finding anyone to do it for free, since I ain't got the budget."

Blue grunted, not quite approving. "You make any progress?"

"Identifying the stranger? No. I've talked to every merchant and innkeeper and saloon man in town. No name."

"What about Castle?"

"He was in here two days before that first murder over toward you. Not in any saloon though. He bought bullets from Jim Schott, the hardware man, that's how I know."

"What caliber?"

"Forty-five. One box."

"He go anywhere else?"

"No. He just drifted in late one afternoon, just a passing stranger, bought bullets, paid with a five-dollar greenback, and drifted out, and no one knew who he was. . . . What about you?"

Blue told him about the dead dog, about tracking Castle into the high country, about finding Tammy's hat—once again. But no sign of Jack Castle.

"He's running circles around me, Zeke. I feel like a pup."

"You need a posse? I could scratch up some men. Mostly blacksmiths, barkeeps, and clerks, though."

"I hate the thought of it coming to that," Blue said. "But that's what it's coming to. He's up there. I want to get him myself. I want him worse than I ever wanted to nab anyone."

Zeke laughed. "He's a smart one. But you'll show him a thing or two, Blue. I've got tipsters all over town. Castle can't ride in here without my learning about it in five minutes. He knows it, too. And if I find out anything, you'll hear of it fast as I can reach you."

"Tammy's going home tomorrow, Zeke. She wants to pick up the pieces."

"You letting her?"

"It's her life. I raised her to live it her way. She's a tough cookie. Who's this man you sent out there?"

"Cletus Parsons? Cowboy, ranch hand. I've used him sometimes as a backup deputy when I'm away. Good head on him. And reliable as long as he's sober, just in case you're wondering. I sent him out there, told him to look after things. He made some deal with Tammy, dollar a day, I guess."

"He's all there is between that killer and Tammy."

Zeke nodded, pulled a bag of Bull Durham and a packet of papers from his pocket, rolled a coffin nail, and lit up with a kitchen match he fired with a thumbnail.

"Like you say, Smiths can take care of themselves," Zeke said. "Tammy's a cat with claws. Anything I can do, call on me."

Blue slept in the hayloft at the livery barn, sharing the place with a boozy cowboy. In the morning he harnessed Tammy's dray horse, hooked it to the spring wagon, and drove the rig to the hotel.

She was waiting. He loaded her in and settled the children.

"Will you be coming?" she asked.

"I'm going to prowl," he said.

"Get him," she said, and surprised him with a buss on the cheek.

"Good bye, Grampa," Joey said.

"You take care of your ma," Blue replied. "She needs some caring."

He watched as Tammy wheeled her rig out of Centerville. Suddenly he felt lonely. He was two days of hard riding from Olivia. He shuffled over to Maisie's Place and spent his last four bits on fried-to-death ham, India rubber eggs, and acid coffee.

He soaked up a quart of the java, studied the local codgers who traded insults each dawn, thought about telling Zeke what he was up to, and decided against it. Blue was a loner. He enforced the law alone and got help only when he had no choice. Anyway, Zeke wouldn't be up. He was a night owl, which was fine because no one had ever heard of a robbery at nine in the morning.

Blue was in a sour mood. Wild goose chases. A smart aleck of a killer who knew Blue all too well and made a mockery of a manhunt. He strolled into an overcast morning, picked at his teeth, and decided to give Tammy a two-hour head start. He would be going out to the Cooper ranch, ghosting along behind, but he didn't want her to know it.

He studied a wanted poster Zeke had nailed to the livery barn; a fairly good likeness of Jack Castle, two-hundred-dollar reward, dead or alive. CONTACT BLUE SMITH, SHERIFF.

Good. Sometimes the posters and dodgers worked. He hoped that damned poster got nailed to every lodgepole pine in the county, and got read by every blue jay and gopher.

Blue's musings didn't lift his spirits any. He saddled Steve Cooper's ranch horse and haltered the buckskin, ignoring the help offered by the hostler, and rode quietly out of town, along that lonely road to Tammy's place. This time he stayed off the path as much as he could, but there were places where land and water hemmed him. He didn't want to be seen this gray day.

He encountered no one that long, lonely trip, a lawman ghosting along, trying not to be seen. Once when a lone rider approached, Blue slipped easily into a willow thicket and waited. It was no one he knew; white haired, probably a half-pensioned old cowboy.

A mile or so from the ranch, Blue cut into a thick stand of timber that rose gradually into the foothills. It was slow going. He worked his way over deadfall and around giant boulders resting darkly in the shade, broke off branches that would have whipped his face, steered into and out of sudden crevasses choked with brush, but he always headed upslope in cover so deep no prying eye would ever see him. He could not say that no ear would ever hear him; working two horses through heavy pine forest was noisy business.

After endless riding, he struck a flat area with aspen, some springs, and tiny parks where deer scat lay thick. With the passage of an hour he reckoned he had climbed five hundred feet and traversed a couple of miles. He was heading for a certain headland overlooking Tammy's ranch, a place to lie down in thick grass and see without being seen.

And there he would guard her, and maybe deliver Jack Castle a surprise.

A while later, while working through dense brush, the ranch horse nickered softly. Dammit!

Blue quit moving. No horse nickered back, and he could only thank the wind for that. Ahead and upwind was some sort of horse.

Blue retreated fifty yards, found a dell where he could picket his horses, and left them there. He edged ahead, careful not to step on a stick, edging closer and closer to that headland with its majestic view over much of the Cooper ranch. He was cautious now. If someone was up there, he wanted to know who.

The forest thinned into brush and grass, and Blue eased ahead, straight into the wind, which helped him. Then as he rounded a boulder, he saw the man. Someone was staring from that headland, someone with a good brass field glass. Someone wearing new ranch clothing, a blue shirt that still had creases where it had been folded, jeans so dark that they had never seen soap and water, a hat still bright and shiny.

Whoever it was stared outward, sitting cross-legged, his back to Blue. Castle, maybe. Castle in new duds, after years in the pen. Castle with that glass, studying the ranch. Castle with a rifle lying in the grass, one with a shiny black barrel and a glowing stock.

Blue eased his revolver from his holster and checked the loads. He had Jack Castle this time, had him good. But Blue was no fool, and spent the next minutes looking for a confederate, checking the brush to either side, seeing what Castle was doing, trying to get the *what* and *why* of it.

He also wanted a gander at Castle's horse; where it was tied, whether there were two. But time ran out. The man stood.

"Lift your hands, don't turn. If you do, I'll kill you," Blue snapped.

The man jerked, and Blue almost shot him.

"Up with your hands! This is the law. Don't touch that rifle."

The man obeyed.

"Don't you move, damn you."

Blue slipped closer; puzzled. This one was too thin for Jack Castle, and vaguely familiar.

Blue moved closer; thirty feet, twenty. Enough.

"Turn around slowly. No fancy moves, if you want to stay alive."

Slowly the man turned around and faced Blue.

Blue felt a jolt run clear through him.

"Absalom, what the hell . . . ?"

His son stood still, hands in the air, waiting gravely.

"You just keep your hands up!" Blue snapped.

Blue circled him, found nothing that bothered him.

"Talk," he snapped.

"Is this how you greet your son?"

"Damn right."

"Let me drop my hands?"

"I'll think about it," Blue said.

"I have nothing to say," Absalom said.

Chapter 15

Absalom stood there, hands up.

"I said *talk*," Blue snapped. He was rattled. He had almost shot his son.

Absalom stood silently.

"What are you doing here?"

"I could ask you the same question."

"Don't get smart with me."

Absalom lowered his arms without invitation. Blue let him. The boy—hell, he was a man now, through pale from the want of sun and weather—stared at his father. He had spent money on an outfit. That was a new beaver hat, new boots, new flannel shirt. And resting in the grass was a shining new Winchester model '73 lever-action repeating rifle. Hanging on a leather cord from the boy's neck were field glasses so big and powerful that the boy could see anything a mile away. Better field glasses than Blue had ever owned, or the county had ever paid for.

A dark suspicion flared through Blue.

"Where's your horse?"

Absalom nodded toward the left.

"Show me."

"Look for yourself."

"I asked what you're doing here."

"Fine greeting I get from my own father."

Blue was tired of this. "Walk in front of me. We're going to the ranch."

"If you're arresting me, name the crime I'm charged with. If not, don't push me around."

"I said march."

But Absalom didn't. Blue itched to lay into the boy, but didn't. This man enraged him, and he didn't know why. His son wasn't doing anything illegal; not that Blue could see. But it was *suspicious*. Yes, that was it: *suspicious*. And that made it Blue's business.

"Tammy know you're here?"

"Ask her."

"I asked you a question."

"And I didn't answer."

Blue could see the pain in his son's eyes. Pain and something more: rage. He deserved to have the hell beaten out of him, sassing his old man like that. But Absalom was twenty-nine, not some boy.

"If you're done with me, then leave me alone."

"Tammy said you were coming and you didn't want your mother or me to know about it."

Absalom was plainly annoyed, but he didn't reply.

Blue circled around this whole thing, itching to get at this. "You know that Steve's dead?"

Absalom nodded.

"How come you know?"

"I watched the funeral."

"Watched the funeral!"

"With these." He pointed to his powerful field glasses.

"So you're sneaking around here, not even letting your sister know you're here. You're seven hundred miles from Denver. What the hell?"

Absalom said nothing.

"I ought to run you in." Blue stared at his son. "You watching over her, is that your notion? You, of all people?"

Absalom didn't reply. Instead, he turned away from his father, settled himself at his place on the headland, and resumed his vigil.

Blue was so mixed up he couldn't sort out his feelings. He was mad. And frustrated. This wasn't a boy he could command, but a man he had not seen in a decade.

"I'm going to use this place. You can go somewhere else," Blue said. "I have business here; you don't."

Surprisingly, Absalom picked up his shining rifle and walked past Blue. The look in his son's eyes was so dark, so hurt, that Blue recoiled from it. There was something terrible happening here, something Blue couldn't deal with.

Blue followed Absalom to his horse, a gray ranch gelding picketed in a dell a hundred yards back. Blue wondered what he expected to see: a copper-colored bay, perhaps? That only made Blue feel worse.

He hated mysteries. After a decade away, his estranged son showed up just when Jack Castle was sprung from the pen.

"Where are you going?" Blue asked.

"I never had a home to go to," his son replied. "And I don't have one now."

Absalom released the horse, slid his Winchester into a new saddle sheath and climbed easily into the new saddle. Then he rode away, deep into the forested slope, until he could no longer be seen.

Blue had rarely known a worse moment.

He walked back to the headland and settled in the exact spot his son had occupied. Down below, Tammy was conversing with a man, probably Cletus. Smoke rose from the bunkhouse where the hired man was staying. Blue itched to have those field glasses so he could see what the hell was going on down there. Why the hell the county didn't give its sheriff some good glasses he didn't know. How the hell could a man enforce the law without a first- rate spyglass? Where the hell did Absalom get enough money to buy lenses like that? Lenses, hell, horse, rifle, saddle, outdoor clothing?

He knew the answer and hated it. The boy was a first-rate artist and engraver, and commanded a good price for all that art stuff he did sitting in some warm office in Denver, working with his fingers. Which irritated Blue. Why the hell didn't he have a son like any other son—a son who could swing an axe?

Well, Absalom would hightail it down to the ranch, greet his sister, settle for some comfortable quarters. Meanwhile there was a killer prowling, a killer whose intent was to destroy Blue's family. Blue settled into the grasses where he could keep an eye on that ranch house far below. Maybe from those hills across the valley Jack Castle was watching and waiting. Blue wished he had those field glasses so he could see. Age was playing hell on his eyesight.

But as an hour slid by, and another, Blue saw nothing more of Absalom. What the hell was all this about? Sneaking around, telling no one. Surveillance was hard, dull work, but Blue was going to keep Tammy safe no matter what. By God, he'd just suffer the boredom and whittle away the hours until he was sure Castle wasn't anywhere around. Or until Castle was manacled or dead.

So Blue sat, letting the summer breezes toy

with his hair, studying the slopes, looking for the serpent in that Eden. He shoved Absalom out of mind; he had the power to do that. Back to Denver, that's where that boy belonged.

He had known plenty of boredom in his days. The badge brought with it a few moments of wild trouble and month after month of sheer boredom, checking doors to see whether they were locked, peering into mercantiles for burglars, writing up reports, feeding drunks after they had slept it off.

At dusk his stomach told him it was time to lay off for a while. The horses needed water. He needed a break. He squinted sharply into the fading light, saw nothing suspect, and then eased back from the headland and plunged into the deep shadows of the forest.

The horses weren't there.

He cursed, peered about, wondered if they had busted loose of their pickets and drifted, and then he saw Tammy's hat, tied by its pink ribbons to the limb where the horses had been, and he knew the horses hadn't drifted. That hat had been tied to his saddle and now it wasn't. Steve Cooper's horses, Blue's saddle and cook pot and slicker and gear: all gone. And the calling card was Jack Castle's.

Blue felt a volcanic rage build in him. He growled, cursed, waved the old Springfield, raged, and clenched his fists.

But there was worse coming. He would have

to hike down the long slope, through the darkling woods, out onto the foothill slopes, and then across lonely fields to Tammy's ranch house, where he would sheepishly ask for still another horse, some chow, and whatever else he needed to outfit himself again.

And then he would stay awake all night, rifle in hand, waiting for that son of a gun to make his move.

Blue started down the slope, stumbling and sliding, and emerged at last upon the lonely meadows. He continued to drop down a long slope following a coulee, and emerged at last on the valley floor. He hoisted himself over the pole fence and into the big horse paddock, and continued toward Tammy's ranch house.

He found the gate and was headed into the ranch yard when he felt cold steel stab his back.

"Stop where you are, mister," said a voice behind him.

"Put that thing down," Blue snarled.

"Hands up. Walk ahead of me."

"I'm the sheriff. Who the hell are you?"

"If you're the sheriff, what are you doing sneaking up on this place?"

"Damn you, put that thing down. I'm going to turn around and show you my star. And then you're going to take me to see my daughter, Tammy. Mrs. Steven Cooper. And if you don't, I'm going to kill you."

"Pretty respectable bellerin' and cussin'," the man said.

"You Cletus?"

The man laughed. "You're her old man, I reckon. All right, I'll put this iron back in its nest."

Blue turned slowly. A lank, rawboned ranch hand contemplated him.

"You want to fix me up with a horse and tack and chow? Real quiet? I want to get out of here unseen."

"I ain't got the right to do that. All I'm doing is feeding stock and shooting strangers." He laughed.

Defeated, Blue headed for the ranch house, wondering what the hell to tell Tammy, and how the hell he could ask for another horse and a saddle, too. Everything had gone wrong that could possibly go wrong.

Chapter 16

Tammy was wearing widow's weeds. How strange she looked in the dim yellow lamplight, all in black, her face ethereally sweet and pale and drawn, the grosgrain tight about her neck, framing her face. His daughter was a widow in her twenties, her home a bleak refuge tossed by a thousand dangers. He looked around for the children but didn't see them.

Absalom stood there, too, his face shadowed, and Blue wondered how the hell his son had arrived unobserved. Hadn't Blue been watching over that house from the headland? Damned boy, sneaking around like that as soon as it got dark.

"What are you doing here?" he asked Absalom, setting the rifle next to the door and tossing Tammy's pink-ribboned hat onto a chair.

Tamara answered, "He's come to visit me, just as I told you he would."

"Oh, yes? Then why was he up on the bluff, snooping around?"

Tammy and Absalom glanced at each other, as if there were something between them that maybe Blue shouldn't know. The moment stretched on and on.

"I would like to show you what I do for my living," Absalom said. He directed Blue's attention to artwork and magazines spread over the kitchen table. *Harper's* and *Leslie's Illustrated Weekly* and a dozen others, plus watercolors, sketches, engravings, and prints mounded high. Blue glanced that way, hating to admit that his son did all that stuff. He stared at superbly rendered images of magpies and hawks and eagles; engravings of moose and deer and elk; watercolors of wolves and big-horned sheep, otters and marmots; bold paintings of longhorns and cowboys herding them; sketches of gunmen holding up a bank, of cowboys being bucked off broncs, of fierce Indians raiding a lonely cabin.

Blue grunted.

Absalom stood expectantly and then sagged, the old hurt on his face again. But Blue didn't care. The boy wasn't strong enough to live in a new land, and he was damned if he'd praise all this desk work.

"Why'd you come now? Why not some other time?" Blue asked him, turning back to the only thing he considered important.

The boy exchanged glances with Tammy again.

"The warden notified me," he said slowly.

"Notified you about what?" Blue felt his bile rising again.

"Long ago I asked him to write me when Jack Castle was about to be released. He did."

"So?"

"So I'm here."

The boy glared at him, daring him to ask more questions. The curtain descended again, and Blue knew he wouldn't get much more out of his son. But maybe Tammy would talk.

"You invited him?"

"Steve and I."

"And now he roams around trying to protect you, as if he could stop Jack Castle."

Tammy's lips compressed. She turned to Absalom. "These are just beautiful, Ab. Would you spare any for me?"

"Any you want. I'm glad you like them. I tried to catch all the things I've seen here."

Blue stood impatiently. They were shutting him out of their conversation. A killer tormenting this family was raging in the hills, and they were talking about that art.

"I need to requisition a horse and tack. Sheriff business," he said.

"A horse? But, Pa . . ."

"There's a killer out there and I need a horse."

"You had two."

"He got them."

"Jack Castle got them?"

"Who else? And right here, up on the hill. He left your hat tied to a tree as a calling card—that hat right there, *your hat*. Is that enough for you? Do you want him to bust in here? Now do I get a horse for sheriff business?"

She stared at her hat, and at him. "And you let him?"

"What do you mean, I let him? I'd've shot him."

"He came within a few yards of you and took two horses, and you let him?"

Blue squirmed. "I didn't hear it."

"Yes, you didn't hear it. Your hearing's not very good, is it? And you need spectacles now, don't you? And maybe he gets across country faster than you."

"That doesn't slow me down a bit. I'm better than ever."

Tamara and Absalom exchanged glances.

"You'll see," he said.

She stared into the night. "I don't know . . . Steve was going to break more. We hardly have a saddle horse left. My mare . . . my side saddle. I think you should rent a horse in town."

"I'll take what I can get." He turned to Absalom. "I need your outfit."

Absalom shook his head. "I don't think so."

"It's official business. I keep the peace, and I'm taking it."

"Maybe Cletus will lend you his."

"I'm taking yours. There's a man out there that's threatening this family, vowed to kill us, hurt us any way he can. Now stand aside."

"No, you don't have my permission."

"I didn't ask your permission."

"Stop that!" Tammy snapped. "You treat your own son like dirt. I won't have it in my house."

Blue started to protest, but Tammy's withering glare gave him pause. He stared malevolently at the citified brother she was protecting, the one with a fancy gray horse and creaking new tack and a shiny rifle bought with his finger fiddling; the horse and tack and rifle that could catch a killer.

"I'll have Cletus drive you to Centerville in the buckboard," Tammy said. "You can deal with your problems there."

"Cletus? There'd be no one here to protect you."

Absalom rocked as if he'd been slapped in the face, but he said nothing.

"Ab and I can protect this place. Go in the buckboard or not. Walk if you prefer."

"I'm trying to protect you," Blue said. "A lot of thanks I get."

Absalom smiled suddenly, unexpectedly, as if there weren't a killer stalking the place. "Pick a few of these for my mother," he said. "Take them with you. She can't see them, but you can tell her what's on the paper. It's a gift to her."

"I don't have time. . . . Oh, hell, you choose some. But if they get wet don't blame me."

Blue couldn't understand why he was picking on Absalom that way. He couldn't let it alone. His own daughter, a new widow, was glaring at him, just when she needed help from him. But if she thought she'd be protected by the likes of that brother of hers in the new box-creased flannels, she had better prepare for the worst. Jack Castle would cut through him like a hot knife in butter.

"Maybe she'll like them drawings," Blue said. That was as close to an apology as he intended to get. "All right. I'll have Cletus drive me, being that's how you feel about it." He turned to Absalom. "How long are you staying?"

"Until my business is done."

"And what's your business?"

His son plunged into silence again. There was something here Blue didn't fathom, and it bothered him. Both Tammy and Absalom stared at him from faces cast in granite. It was as if they had some sort of secret, something they didn't want Blue to know.

"There's something you can do for me, and for yourself," Absalom said. "Deputize me."

"Deputize!"

"You need a deputy here, empowered to uphold the law. Swear me in."

"You? I should deputize Cletus. He's worked for Zeke in town, and he's tough."

His son turned toward the window. "I didn't expect you'd change, and I was right," he said. "That's why I asked Tammy not to let you know I was coming. Or why. You'll always be the same. Nothing will ever change."

"I don't want you shot," Blue said. "Temporary deputy here's a good idea, but it'll be Cletus."

Absalom nodded. There was only bleakness in his face—or was it resignation?

"I'm tired of this," Tammy said. She swung outside, and Blue watched her head for the bunkhouse. Its door opened, flaring light. Moments later Cletus headed for the catch pen and began harnessing a trotter for the buckboard. It would be a long night's ride, but better by night than by day, Blue thought.

Blue spotted some fresh bread in a pie safe, sliced off a piece to hold him until he got some chow, and headed into the gentle night. Tammy was there.

"You mind if I take this?" Blue asked, waving Steve's old rifle.

She shook her head.

That old Springfield felt just fine in his hand.

Cletus drove the buckboard around to the ranch house. It was little more than four spoked wheels on a small box with a hard seat for two. One of its wheels howled on its axle.

"You send for help if you need it," he said to Tammy.

"I have help, Dad."

"Some help."

"Absalom likes city life, but that doesn't mean he didn't learn what you had to teach him. Maybe you should be giving him his due."

"Against Jack Castle? You'll be lucky to live."

"You're the most stubborn and bullheaded man in the county," she said.

"And this is a peaceful place. Or was. If you don't like it, run against me next election."

"Oh!"

Blue got in the last word, as usual, and clambered into the hard seat, knowing his bones would ache by the time he got to Centerville. He laid the old rifle across his lap and nodded to Cletus.

"Wait! You forgot Absalom's gift," Tammy said.

She raced toward the lamplit door of the house and plunged in. Blue sat impatiently, hating to be silhouetted by the lamplight with a wolf out there.

"Just git," he said to Cletus.

"In a moment. I work for her, Sheriff."

When Tammy emerged from the door, she carried a roll of Absalom's artwork wrapped against the rain in a checkered oilcloth.

"You tell Mom this is from him," she said. "And you tell her what each picture is, and good enough so she knows each one. You'll do that? You promise?"

Blue nodded. He hoped the art would get lost en route, and was angry at himself for thinking it. Why was he feeling like a scalded dog?

Chapter 17

Cletus dropped Blue at the livery just before dawn, after a bone-crunching night in the buckboard. Blue stood stiffly in the quiet, knowing that the hostler would have to be aroused. The day's first light backlit the black mountains to the east.

He was tired. He didn't have a dime in his pockets. He had spent half the night wondering what Tammy and Absalom were hiding from him, and had come up with nothing. He felt as sour as a grizzly coming out of hibernation.

He thought of rousting Zeke Dombrowski out of his sack, but thought better of it. The hostler would help. He wandered into the cavernous darkness of the livery barn, smelling newly mown hay, manure, the acrid scent of horses. One whickered at him from a stall. The hostler, a little monkey called Willis, bunked behind the office, which consisted of one battered desk and a stump for a chair.

"Hey, Willis!" he said. "Hey, it's Blue Smith."

He hoped the name would evoke terror and haste in the wiry hostler, but nothing happened.

"Willis, dammit, you come out here. This is the sheriff."

This time he heard muffled rustling within, and pretty soon the door creaked open. Willis, the runt of the litter, lacking only boots, yawned and studied the sheriff.

"What?" he asked.

"It's Blue Smith. I need an outfit fast; right now."

"Day rate?"

"No, buy it."

"You sure? You had coffee yet?"

"Come on now, show me your stock, your tack, and name your price. I'm in a hurry and this is official business."

"Everyone's in a hurry."

Willis vanished into the gloom and emerged with his battered boots encasing his dirty feet. "Hell of a time to buy an outfit," he said. "Don't know that I want to sell. I'm short of riding horses, and all the tack I got is a saddle some cowboy never claimed. Could be he still owns it, once he pays some storage." He eyed Blue. "How about a trotter and a buggy?"

"Saddle horse, and a good one. Good in the

mountains. I'm after someone and every second you fiddle around, he's getting farther away."

"I hear he's after you."

"You can stuff that rumor down someone's throat."

Willis scratched and considered, and led Blue into a catch pen behind the livery barn. He moved easily through the snoozing horses, and slid a halter over a speckled white gelding.

"That your best?"

"He humps up when you get aboard, but you turn him in a circle and he settles. He's a mover."

"He got bad habits?"

"What horse has good habits?"

"Show me the others."

A half hour later, after looking at a lame bay and a mean sorrel that kicked anything within ten feet, Blue settled on the white, along with a slick-forked, single-rigged saddle that would probably bust his butt.

"That comes to one hundred seventy-eight and a half," Willis said.

"I'll draft a voucher on the county."

"Cash."

"I said it's on the county. On the sheriff account, Blankenship Stockmen's Bank."

"County don't pay for six, seven months. Nosiree. You give me your personal warrant, collectable on the Blankenship bank, I'd do her."

"I'm the sheriff, dammit. I tamed this county, and I keep it tame. This is official business, boy. I've kept the peace here since before you were born, boy, and I need a horse."

But Willis wouldn't budge.

Blue penned the personal note, blotted the draft, clambered aboard the white, which shivered under him, and rode into the first sun of the innocent new day.

He rode the white for ten minutes and hated it. Its loopy gait bounced him around and it reined like a plow horse. He started back for the livery barn, thought better of it, and headed toward Blankenship. Years ago, no slicker would have dared to pull a fast one on Sheriff Blue Smith.

He fumed. County was filling up with people who didn't know what Blue Smith had done to tame the place, and worse, who didn't care. Maybe he would show them a thing or two now that wild Jack Castle was prowling. Maybe they'd think twice about crossing Blue Smith or unloading bad horseflesh. Time was he'd ask for a horse and they'd bring him the best there was in the area, anything to help old Blue. But that was long ago.

The hostler couldn't come up with a saddle sheath, so Blue had to tie the old Springfield down with saddle strings and hope he didn't have to use it, because it would be a devil to untie in a hurry.

He would get a proper outfit in the county seat, peddle this nag to a rendering company, and hang the expense on the county, like it should be. And then he'd fetch a noose around Jack Castle's thick neck, that's what. He rode through a fine, cool morning, following the road to Blankenship, which described a long loop around the mountains that lay between the towns. He scared up crows and magpies, pushed the addled white horse through meadowlands and cottonwood groves, stopped at a sweet-water spring to rest and listen to meadowlarks, and then rode the lumbering nag onward. There was nothing worse than a bad horse, and he cursed Willis with every passing mile. But it was a fine sunny day, not too hot, dew on the grass, and the horse was eager; he could say that for it. It beat a nag he had to spur and whip.

Ahead a horseman awaited him, tight-reining a hot-blooded black that wouldn't stand still. The man waved lazily, wanting to visit, and Blue put heels to his lumbering white steed. The man wore fringed buckskin pants, a blue flannel shirt, red neckerchief, and a flat-crowned, cream-colored hat. Pretty flashy dresser, but the young were like that.

Blue reined up, and knew suddenly it was too late.

The snout of a blue steel revolver bored at his chest, and behind it sat Jack Castle, grinning easily. He was a handsome son of a gun; chiseled face, clear green eyes that laughed, and an easy way about him. Blue felt a rush of terror and admiration.

"Sweating a little, Blue? Imagine so. Think you just bought it, eh? I would too, was I in your boots. There he is, old Jack Castle, not good enough for your family, too wild for a nice girl like Tammy, pointing forty-five hundredths of an inch of lead at your chest."

Blue steadied the horse. A man busy talking was a man not shooting. But Blue figured his days were done, and there was no way out.

"Surprised, Blue? I suppose you are. Here's old Jack, standing in the middle of the main road where he's not supposed to be. Old Jack's supposed to be running from Blue Smith, running clear to California, hiding out from the law. And here he is, fresh out of the pen, and there you are, king of the county, just like always."

Blue felt his pulse rise. The bore of that six-gun never wavered.

"Look at that old Navy. Real easy now, Blue, unbuckle that belt and let it drop."

Blue did as directed. His belt, holster, and revolver slid into the clay.

"Now, Blue, you untie those saddle strings and lower that old army rifle of Steve's down, real careful how you point the muzzle. Darndest thing to be toting around, ten extra pounds of iron. Funny how a sheriff arms himself these modern days."

"I guess I won't," Blue said. "Do it yourself."

The shot startled him. Blue felt lead sear past his ear. He slowly undid the Springfield with trembling fingers and let it slide.

"Now, you empty your pockets of those old army cartridges, Blue."

Blue pulled each pocket inside out and let the contents fall.

"That's better. Now, Blue, we'll have a little discussion."

"It's going to be one-sided. I've nothing to say to you."

Castle grinned, baring even white teeth. "Poor old Blue, getting chased all over the mountains by an outlaw just out of the pen, trying to figure out what's next. But you really know what's next. Sitting there, wondering if you're breathing your last, whether you'll see the sun rise again."

Castle was toying with him. Blue hunkered low inside of himself, looking for the break. Even men as skilled as Jack Castle made mistakes.

"You're not going to die yet," Castle said. "Not for a while. Not until you see what happens."

"What's going to happen?"

"You'll know soon enough, Sheriff. For years I've been thinking on it. Thinking, hell, I've worked it out, Blue, worked out all the ways that a hard old man who thought his daughter was too good for me can feel pain. When I'm done, you'll know what it's like to be on the receiving end."

Something violent built up in him, chilling Blue. "Everything that's going to happen to you, it's nothing compared to what you did to me. You're going to take it, and there isn't a thing you can do about it. You wrecked my life, and you'll see what it's like.

"How about a posse, Blue? You're too proud to depend on one and you know I'd make fools of the whole lot. I'll brag. I'm better than ever, Blue. I'm young; you're not. Go ahead and lay traps, comb the mountains, outguess me. Go right ahead. Wire every sheriff hereabouts. Get up a few posses. Start a big snipe hunt. Converge on me from all sides. It'll be amusing. I'm exactly what you wish Absalom could be. Poor pale devil, guarding his fine, respectable, virtuous sister from the likes of me. I'm the son you couldn't have, isn't that right?"

"No, Jack, I always wanted an honest son."

"Even now you're sitting there, cursing yourself for missing that coulee there. See how it stretches north into the mountains? That's how I got here; rode fifteen miles down that gulch to this road. It's my highway into the high country. This is where I robbed that stagecoach, but you forgot that, didn't you? Back when you were a real sheriff and not a husk of one, you'd have seen it, seen what a gulch like that might mean, and I wouldn't have caught you unprepared, easy pickings, a man living in his past and too proud, too blind, and too deaf to respond."

Blue listened carefully, miserably, knowingly. But another part of him was searching, weighing. He would live, for the moment. And that was all he asked.

"Take a good look, Blue. Look at me. All those years behind bars. Not years, Blue—months, days, weeks, hours, minutes, *seconds*. They do things to you. They make you hate. I'm a hater, Blue. They make you mean. I'm mean, Blue, and you'll see how mean a man can get. Meaner than anything you've ever seen. It's not just freedom they take away; it's who you are, too. It's like a tattoo on the forehead the rest of your life. That's what you did."

Blue thought for a moment that Castle would pull the trigger, but then the killer look slid from the man's face.

"All right, Blue, off that plug. And then hang the belt over the saddle horn. Go ahead: Try something fancy if you want. I'd enjoy it. And then start walking. Blankenship's only thirty miles."

Blue slid to the ground, feeling pain shoot up his stiff legs, and carefully hung the revolver belt over the horn.

"Walk," Castle said.

But Blue walked straight toward Castle, straight into that black bore, his rage barely contained. Walked toward that tight-reined horse. Walked toward his quarry. Walked with intent. One yank of the bridle and he'd have Castle; he was that close to ending it all.

"Stop, Blue." Castle's voice was low and deadly.

Blue didn't. He put one foot forward, and then another, until he was close enough to grab that bridle and start that jittery horse pitching. Only then did Castle back the horse. And that's when Blue saw the flare of something, maybe fear, in Castle's eyes.

"Damn you, Blue!"

The shot seared past Blue's ear.

Blue stopped cold.

"Turn around and walk."

Blue walked. Then he looked back. Castle had picked up the rifle and was riding up the coulee leading the white horse. Funny thing. He didn't care about the white plug or Steve Cooper's old Springfield or his revolver, or the slick-forked saddle or the rest of his gear. He felt bad about losing Absalom's art, the boy's gift to his blind mother.

Chapter 18

Deputy Carl Barlow was grinning, and that made Blue mad. It was bad enough having to confess to his underling that he'd had four horses shot or stolen from him, along with his own outfit and another belonging to his daughter. Worse still, Jack Castle had held him up and casually made off with the last of his possessions, including a borrowed rifle. And here was his own damned deputy grinning at him.

"Wipe that smile off your face. We're dealing with a killer."

Barlow slowly erased the grin and ran a hand through wiry red hair. "Olivia took it hard, losing Steve Cooper. I read her that letter, and I couldn't comfort her."

"I haven't been there yet. I've been sitting in a freight wagon for two damned days."

That had been another offense to his person, hitching a ride with a teamster driving an ox-drawn freight wagon at ten or twelve miles a day. But his stiff old legs wouldn't take the thirty-mile hike after Castle set him afoot.

"How's she been, other than that?" Blue asked, dreading the answer.

"Hell, Blue, she didn't get locked up to sleep anything off."

"But she was sampling?"

"Sure. She always does when you're on the loose. She's got her a little green mason jar left over from canning beans she takes into Finnigan's and lays out some coin, and then she goes to the park after dark and sips and cusses at dogs. I saw her there ten times maybe, and I just left her alone. She gets ornery, you know, beggin' your pardon."

"Not around me she doesn't. It's just that you don't know how to keep her respectful. Me, I keep everyone respectful, starting with my own wife."

Barlow was grinning again, damn his pasty hide.

"Did it get into the paper again?"

"No, but the county commissioners told me they were going to cut the sheriff budget."

"Because of her?"

"They're politicians, Blue. Levers, that's all they think about. Sheriff has a wild woman, so they can cut his budget."

"I gotta get a new outfit. Mine got took in the

line of duty. And I'm going to bill them for the Cooper ranch horses that got stolen."

Barlow was laughing again, and that was too much for Blue.

"I'm going home. You're enjoying my misery."

"I'll make a campaign issue of it, Blue. Economy in office. What kind of sheriff goes through a dozen horses?"

"Lay off."

Blue stormed out into a hot July afternoon. He didn't want to face Olivia. He didn't want to tell her about Absalom and his art and his furtive visit to Tammy's ranch for reasons unclear. He didn't want to confess that so far, his entire effort to catch Jack Castle had come to ruin. But he would.

He hiked the three blocks to his cottage. The lilacs had quit but the pink peonies were still blooming and the yellow roses were rioting and the hollyhocks were about to. The front door was never locked, and he opened it.

"Blue!"

He found Olivia peering out a window, loving the golden light, which was all she saw. Pearly light she called it, from a midday window.

He hugged her as she rose, liking the sweetness of her tugging arms, the warm solidness of her body, the curves that still stirred him, the gentle hands that were measuring him as she saw him with her fingers.

"Bad this time," she said at last. "You're tired."

"Worse than that. I haven't got him. And he cleaned me out of everything I own and borrowed."

"You hungry?" she asked.

"Later, Olivia." He pulled her to the horsehair sofa and sat her down, sliding her hand between his rough ones. "You behaved yourself?"

"As little as possible," she replied.

"Barlow says he'll campaign on it."

She laughed. "He told me not to let the dogs get close."

"Olivia . . . We've got a killer loose, and he's threatening this family. I think he's still got an eye for Tammy, and that worries me plenty."

"Tell me about Steve, Blue. Everything there is."

Blue did, describing a cold murder, done to torment Blue and his family. Little by little he told her, coughing up the story and his failures like phlegm and spitting them out, each hated event—losing horses, losing gear, dealing with Castle's threats, the hat with the pink ribbons, and, finally, the moment when Castle, the most wanted man in the county, casually intercepted Blue on the main road, took another horse out from under Blue, warned him what was coming, and rode off.

"I'm going to get him, going to get him," Blue muttered, but for the first time he wondered whether he would.

"It'll get worse," she said, holding his hand.

"What do you mean?"

"Much worse, Blue."

"You seeing things again?"

She closed those blind eyes, and he swore she shuddered.

"I'll get him. I'll find a way," he said, not knowing what way.

"Is Tammy all right? Foolish question."

"She's tough."

"What aren't you telling me, Blue?"

She had found him out. She always did.

"Absalom," he said. "Damned boy."

"I knew, I knew," she said.

"You knew?"

"That he would come to us."

"To Tammy, not to us. To protect her, that's what I make of it. He kept in touch with the warden, and when Castle was freed, he went to protect her and Steve. As if he could protect anything."

"Don't, Blue."

"He bought himself a shiny outfit, and when I found him he was up on the mountain with a new rifle watching over the ranch. Now, why would he do that? What does he know about Castle that I don't know?"

"Maybe a lot."

Blue grunted. He still had some bad business ahead and decided to get it over with. "He's some kind of artist. Mostly engravings for those fancy magazines, but other stuff too. Wildlife from around here, cowboys, livestock, stuff like that."

"Is he good?"

Blue stopped what he was about to say about finger-fiddling. "Yes, he's good," he said. "Best I've seen."

She touched Blue's cheek.

It all came out, as if Blue were sawing off his own fingers: Absalom's gift to her, Blue's promise to describe each picture in detail so she might see it within herself, Castle's theft.

"I guess that's pretty hard news, those pictures all wrapped in an oilcloth for you, and now Jack Castle's got them. He's probably using them to start fires."

She was crying. She had borne Steve Cooper's death, the threats, Blue's losses. But this stolen gift of unseen and unseeable art from her estranged son was too much, and she sat rigidly, not stopping the tears that rolled down her weathered cheeks.

He couldn't stand tears, and bolted upright, prowling the parlor. That damned boy had opened up a vein. Why the hell did he come out here, upsetting Olivia's world like that?

"Anyway, he's not coming here," he said. "He's just causing trouble. And he's likely to get himself hurt if he thinks he's a match for Jack Castle."

But that only made it worse, and Blue clammed up suddenly.

"What did he say?" she asked at last.

"We didn't talk. He takes offense at me. He kept telling me I haven't changed. As if he expected me to."

"He must have said something about why he's there."

"Yes. He asked the warden to notify him, and he took off from his work when he heard. Why the hell he'd do that I don't know. Him and Tammy, they've got something between them they're not telling."

Olivia stood slowly. "It had to come," she said.

He didn't know what the hell she was talking about.

But she was heading for the kitchen, navigating with her internal compass toward the bread box. She would soon have a cold summer supper for him, as effortlessly as if she had her vision.

"What is Jack like?" she asked, cutting cold beef, feeling her way along with her fingers.

"He'll make a mistake," Blue said.

"Is he still . . . like a son?"

"He never was."

"Is he different?"

"You don't stay the same in the pen. He put a bullet an inch from me."

"How are you going to get him?"

"I almost did, on the road. I almost by God got him by just walking up there and taking him. I almost yanked him off that horse. I saw him hesitate. With him, it's just challenge is all. He's not making himself scarce, he's not escaping, not fleeing the country. He's here, looking for trouble, so I'll let him look."

"I'm afraid, Blue."

"Don't be."

"He's worse now. Before, it was devil-may-care. Now there are no rules, nothing to slow him."

"He knows one rule: fear. I saw it, and I'll use it."

She slid a cold beef sandwich before him, and he masticated it slowly, using his remaining incisors on the meat.

Her hand slid over his shoulder, across his back, seeing him with her fingers. It was an invitation.

Chapter 19

The next morning Blue got into a fight.

"Four horses and a mule!" County Supervisor Abe Clayborne yelled, "Two saddles, tack, a rifle, a shotgun, and a slicker! And you want *us* to pay?"

Blue stood stiffly, miffed at that attitude. He hated this. "Lost in the line of duty."

"That's half your annual budget."

"I want a horse. Hector got shot. Your peace officers need horses, and spares and pack animals, and that's that. You want me to protect this county without a horse? Sit here and whittle on a stick?"

Clayborne shook his head. "I won't do it. This claim from your daughter—two horses—I won't do it."

"I got two horses from Cooper Ranch in the line of duty; both got stolen. A rifle too. A peace officer can't just walk off with property. I owe her."

Blue was getting heated. Begging was unbearable. Clayborne was a pinchpenny.

"It'll come out of your salary, Blue."

"No, it won't. You'll buy me some horses and square it with my daughter, and work it into the county budget."

"It'll come out of your jail budget, Blue. I'll get you one horse and it'll come out of your jailbird food allotment."

"The hell it will."

Clayborne looked pained, the sort of daily pain caused by hemorrhoids. "Buy one damned horse," he croaked, "and don't pay more than a hundred fifty, and find some used tack somewhere. And if it rubs you raw there's a lesson in it; it's your ass, and you can feed your jailbirds pinto beans for the next fiscal year."

"I'll get them horses back. He's got them up there somewheres," Blue said. "How about I rent a horse and saddle from the livery barn for a few weeks?"

"At two dollars a day? Piracy. And who's to say you'll get any horses back? Who's to say Jack Castle's in the territory?" The supervisor looked as if he were just stepping out of a two-holer. "Buy one horse and that's it. You lose it and Barlow's taking over. He's got three, four horses, and he don't lose them or get them shot."

"Fine way to treat a man that's given thirty years of his life to keeping the peace around here."

One horse, anyway.

Blue headed for a certain boozy horse broker he knew, a man as crooked as he could get away with when dealing with widows and ministers but straight with Blue most of the time, and willing to dicker.

Smooth Eddie operated on the south side of Blankenship and always had a dozen or so nags in his string. Blue hiked over there, found the horses in a paddock, and wandered through. He wanted a look at all that horseflesh before Smooth began his sweet talk and passing the bottle back and forth.

But Smooth Eddie saw him coming, and by the time Blue put a boot to the split-rail fence, Eddie was right there, lipping a skinny cigar.

"I'll cut right to it," Blue said. "I need a horse, and the county's springing for only a hundred and a half, and that's it. I want a three-hundred-dollar horse for half price, and he better move fast and keep on going all day, because that's all I'll buy."

Eddie lipped his cigar. "I'll sell you the rear half for that and give you a mortgage on the front half."

"I don't have time to waste."

"Then you'll end up picking a dog."

"You don't have dogs in your string."

Smooth Eddie chortled. He eyed his herd and pointed at a red roan. "That one," he said.

"What's wrong with him?"

"Nothing. He's green and flighty. Needs a sheriff on him to settle down. Some Blue Smith authority."

"How old?"

"Three, and started. Joe Kingsley started him."

"That's all I need—a horse I can't control when I'm in a jackpot. How much for a blanket, saddle, and bridle with him?"

"Two hundred puts you on that horse."

Blue climbed onto the roan, walked, trotted, loped, and galloped. Liked the gelding even if he was half broke. Then he studied the legs and chest and stifles, looked for cracked hooves, checked the frogs and pasterns, ran a hand down each leg, lifted the horse's lips, looked for worms, ran a hand along the withers looking for fistulas, studied the horse's eye, which was gentle and bright, and he bought.

"Bill the county," he said.

"I will, but you'll just sign a little note saying if the county don't cough up, you're liable."

Blue fumed and signed. He rode back into Blankenship, liking the eager movement of the roan. This nag would take him to Castle up there in the mountains. Life wasn't so bad.

He tied it to the jail hitch rail. Barlow was sitting on the bench outside, whittling.

"New nag?"

"Smooth Eddie's best."

Barlow laughed. "We'll see."

"I'm going fishing."

"You been away. Mail piled up on your desk sky high, three, four, letters, I think, and a Monkey Ward catalogue. Two ladies of the night in the pen, got into a catfight. Some dodgers you ain't looked at, vouchers, and a killer's loose."

"That's why I'm going fishing. This started at my fishing hole, and I'll end it there. Castle knows where to find me. He's the one doing the man-hunting now."

Barlow quit whittling. "You want help?"

"No, you just look after things. Check on the missus now and then."

"When'll you be back?"

"Tonight. I got to break in this strawberry horse. But I'm going out again tomorrow, and I'm going fishing every day until Castle comes snooping around, because he knows I'm there, and I'll be waiting with a few surprises, and it'll be over. It's like reeling in a fat cutthroat, Carl."

"Cutthroats can't kill you," he said, and spat.

Blue entered the gloomy office, ransacked it for a saddle sheath and an old shotgun, poured a few twelve-gauge buckshot cartridges into his pockets, and left the mess to Carl Barlow.

He stopped at his house long enough to collect his collapsible bamboo rod and reel and creel, and an ancient canvas vest loaded with pockets stuffed with hooky little flies, and then steered the strawberry toward the mountains. The morning's heat was already oppressive and enervating, but Blue knew that altitude would bring some cooler air.

He was thinking about those fish, lazily lording over the fishing hole, staying put with an occasional flip of their fins—fish he hadn't had time to catch for weeks now, fish just waiting for him, especially now with the water running clear after the spring runoff.

"I'm coming, Castle," he said, wondering why he said it when he was thinking about a private pool full of cutthroats.

The fishing hole was where it started and where it would end because Castle couldn't leave it alone. Blue concentrated on the roan, giving the horse gentle instruction in neck-reining, heel signals, knee signals. A young horse like that learned quick. He'd never be as good as old Hector, but he'd be good, and Blue figured he was lucky to get that sort of horseflesh out of Smooth Eddie.

The gelding took Blue up the narrow trails, and gradually Blankenship dropped behind him and the air turned sweet again. He paused at the crest of the wooded divide that sealed the fishing hole from the world, and studied the place from the shadows. The grasses shimmered in the noon sun. The creek rippled unperturbed. He watched mountain bluebirds flit. The waters of the hole looked deep and cold.

The place was a trap. Castle could settle anywhere around the rim of that sunny basin and wait with a rifle. But that wasn't Castle's style; the punk would let Blue know first. Blue rode down the wooded trail until he burst into the meadowed bottoms fragrant with the scent of sun-hammered pines.

He picketed the strawberry roan close in, plucked the shotgun from its sheath, studied the old fishing hole, and knew he would catch a good string before riding back. If he boned and filleted them, Olivia would fry them for supper.

Soon he had his rod assembled, a red-tailed fly on the line, and a place picked out and the shotgun one step away. He was fishing for cutthroats and killers.

Blue sat down at his favorite place, a rocky flat overlooking the deep and mysterious waters, and let the breezes wash over him. He peered into the dark pool. In just the right light he could see seven or eight feet down into that crystal water.

There was Big Eye. He was sure of it; the great-grandfather of all trout, lazily eyeing Blue. He had caught Big Eye several times and always let him go, because he put up the best fight in all the holy and finny kingdom of fish. He could always spot Big Eye, who had abnormally large and black eyes, eyes different from any fish he had ever caught. And there he was, ready for a fight. Big Eye liked the fight as much as Blue, and half the time spit out the hook and flipped away, giving Blue a final contemptuous wiggle before vanishing into the deeps of that pool.

"All right, come to me, Big Eye. What are you biting this hot day, eh?"

Blue stood, feeling the sun bake his back and neck, feeling the flexing rod in his hand, the long black line spun in England. He had gotten everything from England, where they knew all about trout. It was time to reel in Big Eye. He whipped his line until it soared, and whipped it back and out and then farther out until it dropped that red-tailed fly right over Big Eye, right where he had always caught Big Eye.

The monster didn't even wait. He was up, out, clamping the fly in his hard jaws, and racing for the deep on Blue's first cast, as if to tell the sheriff he had missed him. Blue's reel sang, and the line raced down, down, down into that dark pool, and Blue let Big Eye run.

Then it was over. The line went slack. Blue reeled it in, and found nothing on the end. He felt cheated. Big Eye was good for twenty minutes of sheer joy. He rummaged around in his vest, looking for a new leader and fly, and soon had himself in shape, but the afternoon was ruined. Big Eye was sulking down there, out of sight, and unwilling to come out and fight.

time to go, Blue reeled in his wet line and disassembled his rod and stored it on the strawberry roan. He gutted his fish and packed them in cold, wet grass for the trip home. Olivia knew exactly how to salt and season and fry them, and they would have a fine trout fillet supper that night, as they often did. But it would never be the same, and he sorrowed.

He steered the young horse up the forest path and over the ridge, looking back this time on his erstwhile paradise and feeling he had lost a kingdom. Then he hurried the horse downslope. His thoughts were on that dead stranger, who remained unidentified in spite of a massive effort by all the lawmen in the area.

Had Castle anything against the man, or was he murdered simply because he was nearby and convenient? Had Castle reached the point of depravity that he would murder a man just for sheriff bait, a man with his own dreams and family and hopes? A man who had done Castle no harm?

Blue knew the answer.

He rode into Blankenship after the time most folks took supper—they didn't call it dinner in these parts—but Olivia would be used to that. The long summer's light often delayed Blue's return from the mountains. He unsaddled the strawberry roan in the carriage barn in the back, brushed and fed him, gathered his gear and creel, and headed for the door of his shadowed cottage.

"Olivia?" he said, as he entered. No light burned; she didn't need a flame eating at a wick.

She didn't reply. He set down the creel at the zinc sink and headed for the parlor.

She lay on the floor, face up, her throat cut from ear to ear, having bled only a little. Her mouth was primly shut. Her milky eyes gazed at nothing. Beside her, on the oak library table, rested the roll of Absalom's paintings and etchings and woodcuts, still wrapped in checkered oilcloth. A great silence filled the house.

Blue felt weak at the knees, his strength flowing away from him.

"Olivia, no," he said. "No."

He steadied himself, for he could not walk and could not stand because his legs failed him. He made it to the place where she lay, on the Brussels carpet, waxen and lifeless. He took her hand. Not all the heat had left it.

"Olivia," he said, "I should have stayed."

He slumped on the floor beside her, holding her hand, while the shadows lengthened across the room as the sun died. He had not thought of her death before; he knew he would die before she did. He knew she would come visit him in the graveyard and trace the inscription on the stone with her fingers, and leave him a bouquet.

But it wasn't like that now. His cottage, with the lilacs and roses, was ash.

He took a great gulp of air and tried to stand, but couldn't, having felt his body age twenty years in a few seconds. But he stood at last, not knowing what to do, not wanting Carl Barlow here profaning this place, not wanting to talk to that damned Vinegar Will or the coroner Prentiss or Cyrus Meek or anyone else. He didn't want to sit through a funeral or any of that. He didn't want Vinegar Will laying his dirty hands on her, even to get her fixed up in the coffin.

Blue stood stupidly, unable to move.

It had been so easy. Castle walked in, probably talked with her, and she would have known who it was. Probably he just talked and then walked around behind her with a sharp knife and cut the jugulars, and so she died. And he probably walked away from this residential street, unnoticed in sleepy Blankenship, until he reached his horse and quietly disappeared. Somehow he had read Blue's mind, knew Blue was fishing, knew that murder could be done easily, knew how to torment Blue the most.

Blue stood dizzily, the blood gone from his head. He had to get help. He had to let Tammy know, and Absalom, too, let them know, tell them that their mother, who'd rocked their cradles and fed them ten thousand meals, had been murdered, and by the man who had murdered Tammy's husband—and all because of him, Blue, the sheriff who thought Castle wasn't right for his daughter.

He walked heavily out the door, walked down the quiet street toward the courthouse where Barlow might or might not be, it being the supper hour still. Walked, one foot forward, then the next, carrying more burden than any man should ever carry.

Barlow wasn't there, and Blue didn't mind. That gave him another few moments before the world knew. Barlow would be supping at the Silver Slipper, and that was a block away, and that meant Blue's grief would be his private business for two more minutes.

He found Barlow sipping java.

"You were going to look after her," he said.

Barlow looked up, blankly.

"You didn't look after her."

"What's eating you, Blue?"

"She's dead."

Barlow unfolded from his chair. "Olivia? Dead?"

"Damn you."

Half the patrons were staring but Blue didn't care. He motioned Barlow out the door and into the gloomy street.

"He came and killed her."

By now Barlow was running, and Blue could hardly keep up on his old legs. It winded him to run like that. Barlow got ahead, and Blue quit because his legs wouldn't take him there.

When he got to the cottage Barlow was standing in the dark parlor, staring.

"Blue, God, Blue."

"Well, cover her up. Call Vinegar. Call Prentiss."

The deputy knelt beside the still form and took Olivia's hand, stiff now and cold. He cried, and that made Blue itch.

"I got home, few minutes ago, and this . . ."

Barlow stood slowly and peered about. "What's that, Blue?" he asked, spotting the oilcloth.

"Castle's calling card. Those are Absalom's art wrapped up in there. Which Castle got when he took my outfit. He's just making sure I know he did it, leaving it there."

"What do you think happened?"

"What I think happened was that you weren't watching."

Barlow sagged and then straightened. "I walked past here once. I was coming again after supper."

"You should have just about camped here."

Barlow swallowed a retort, and then set to work. "Blue, you sit here and wait. I've got to get help." He touched Blue's shoulder, his fingers gentle. Blue felt the touch, and felt ready to crumple. Wearily, Blue settled in the morris chair and waited in the gloom while Barlow rounded up the ones he needed.

Blue knew he had been hard on the deputy.

Too hard. Blue had a sore-toothed feeling. Jack Castle had killed his wife, danced around him as if he were a punch-drunk boxer, and who would be next?

Blue didn't keep track of time; he knew only that time passed and then the room was full of people, and some of them were trying to be kind, and he didn't want their kindness.

He should have stayed home instead of gone fishing. He should have looked after her, with that killer running around, looked after her and not trusted the likes of Barlow. Sat there in the parlor with his revolver in his lap instead of trying to catch Big Eye.

He thought all those things and they didn't work. He didn't believe his own thoughts, so he stopped and stared as Dr. Prentiss wrote out a certificate, Barlow wrote up a report, and then Vinegar and his moronic flunky lifted Olivia—lifted his wife, and all too familiarly too—onto a stretcher and hauled her out to his Black Maria.

He would go on down to Vinegar's place when he was ready. Make some damned arrangements. Try to think what Olivia would want. He'd never given it a thought. She had never said. He might have to buy a lot in the boneyard and put up a stone, and where the hell he could find money for that he didn't know. But she'd get the best money could buy.

There was no telegraph between Blankenship

and Centerville. If he expected Olivia's daughter and son to attend the services, he would have to send a rider to her ranch; seventy miles of hard going. And they'd have to catch the thrice-weekly stagecoach, a mud wagon with open sides, actually. Maybe get to town on Friday. Vinegar would know what to do. Barlow would know someone to send. Barlow should get in touch with Zeke Dombrowski, too, put a guard on that coach, shoot any son of a gun that tried to stop it. The boy wouldn't be worth diddly squat in a jackpot.

Damned Barlow; why didn't he walk past that house once, two or three times an hour? He should have, with a killer on the loose like that.

Blue settled into his morris chair with a shawl over his knees and the old shotgun across his lap, and there he sat into the night, into the blackness. The house wasn't the same. The fishing hole wasn't the same. He'd been married to the same woman most of his life, and they hardly used words anymore because they talked to each other without them. Nothing was the same anymore, and he was getting old, and Barlow should be sheriff now. But not yet. Not until the unfinished business was done.

Blue whacked his big, rough fist into the cold wooden arm of the chair, and hurt himself.

Chapter 21

Blue hated funerals so much he thought he would have to handcuff himself to the chair. He had seen plenty of death. It was the ceremony he couldn't deal with.

Vinegar had taken over, gotten a preacher, made the arrangements. Blue scarcely knew any preachers; that had been Olivia's department. He didn't deal with things he didn't understand, and religion was one of them. He had a sense of God, and God's world out at the fishing hole, but not religion.

He sat in the front row, Tammy and Absalom beside him, and itched. The man was saying that now Olivia could see; on earth she had been without vision but in paradise everything was crystal clear. That was fine, but Blue could barely sit. He fumbled with the handcuffs that rested in the pocket of his single suit, ready to, by God, snap them over the chair arm and his wrist if it came to that. He would, by God, make himself sit through it.

There beside him was Absalom, back in Blankenship after a decade, less pale now than when he arrived. And there was Tammy, two deaths now, husband and mother, sitting sternly. Not just deaths. *Murders.* The children were being cared for back at the house.

His son and daughter had come on the stagecoach without incident. Absalom said little, but something burned in his eyes, and Blue sensed that the young man was not saying much about what was going on in his head. Tammy was the one who seemed fearful now; wilted and afraid that the Smith family's suffering was not over, and maybe had scarcely begun. They had barely talked; Blue's taciturnity had discouraged it.

Half of Blankenship had come; most of them because they loved Olivia, some out of curiosity, a few because they pitied Blue. Murder enthralled them. But none came because they loved old Blue, that was for sure. He would have arrested them on sight for getting moony about it all.

Mostly he just ached. She was gone. He missed her. It was so simple. It didn't require theology. There was nothing profound about it. She was dead.

They took her in an ebony hearse with black pom-poms on it out to the boneyard, where a hole had been sawed into the hard clay. There under a grim gray sky they lowered the pine box into the ground, and the preacher offered another prayer.

Blue listened, granite faced, nothing playing across his features except an occasional hard-eyed squint toward the mountains where Jack Castle roamed and was probably celebrating.

Then people solemnly shook his hand or patted him on the back, and drifted away. All except a dozen who lingered; men of consequence in Blankenship, standing around like penguins.

"Blue," said Wiley Gillespie, "we're thinking maybe it's time to send out a posse."

So that was it. Blue stiffened. "I'll get him myself," he said.

"It's not just between you and Castle," Gillespie continued, resuming a much-rehearsed argument. "Castle's endangering the whole area—here, Centerville, the entire territory. He's mocking the law and the peace. This is a public matter. Castle murdered a stranger in cold blood, not just your people. We think it's time to put together a few dozen able men and clean him out of those mountains before he . . . rampages again. What if more innocents die? What of the children? There's frightened children in this county; children whose mothers won't let them out of their yards. Blue, every man and woman in the county's worried, some are terrified, and not a one thinks that you should be doing this alone. You alone aren't enough to protect us. There's even talk of getting the militia."

Blue stared at those earnest faces and those black suits, and the gold watch fobs and wilted collars and paisley cravats, and the black silk top hats and the boiled white shirts.

"A posse costs money," he said, striking at their jugulars.

"Justice and safety are paramount," Gillespie said. "The commissioners are unanimous. It's not just you against that killer. They'll spend."

Blue saw how it was going. He could tell them a thing or two about Jack Castle, who would laugh at posses and play jokes on them. Castle was the best wilderness man in the West, except maybe Blue himself.

"All right," Blue said. "Get your men together for the deputizing. I'll send out Barlow and as many men as the county wants."

"We're thinking forty, in two groups," Gillespie said.

Blue nodded. "Done," he said. "Have them at the office in an hour."

"Make it two hours," Gillespie said. "You get some rest, and let Carl Barlow handle this, Blue."

Blue watched the town fathers drift away. They were sure they were going to get results. There were tough men in Blankenship, men who had settled a wilderness, survived the wild mining camps, dealt with Indians and road agents and the ferocity of nature. Relentless trackers, men who had lived in rough weather, men with bullet wounds on their bodies.

Maybe they would catch Jack Castle. But Blue knew they wouldn't unless Castle made a freakish mistake. Jack Castle could walk right through their midst without being seen. They could put hound dogs or bloodhounds on Jack Castle, and they wouldn't get a whiff of him.

They could put the best horseflesh on Castle's trail and Castle would outrun them and keep his mount fresher. They could shoot at him and hit nothing, and lie dying from Castle's own lead. Still, if the town fathers wanted a posse, Blue had no objection. They were right: It wasn't just between Blue and Castle.

Two hours later he deputized the whole lot and stood silently as they rode out of town, thirty-five temporary lawmen who would be at each others' throats in a day or two and quitting a day after that.

"We'll see if this works," Barlow said. "It's for you, Blue. Castle, dead or alive."

Blue nodded.

They were heading toward his fishing hole, and that made his gut churn. That was his turf.

He discovered himself alone on this burial day. Tammy and Absalom were receiving people at the house. That suited Blue fine; he would have had to handcuff himself to the morris chair to survive that.

Old Will Parker was at the jail keeping house. Will had been a lawman once, in the old days. Tough one, too, even with a shot-up elbow. Now he helped out sometimes; acted as jailer when they had someone locked up, filled in. Carl had gotten him out of retirement.

"Will, I'm heading out. You're going to be the law around here for a while. You up to it?"

Will chewed on his plug for a moment. "I reckon."

"Then put on that badge in the drawer. You're sworn."

"Where you going?"

"I don't know."

"Reckon that's as good a place as any."

Blue's outdoor clothes were in the house, but he didn't want to go back there, not to all that kindness and sympathy and concern and love. He would just about drown in it.

Instead he collected an outfit out of the jail, as well as a shotgun, an old Navy revolver that was lying in a drawer, some powder, balls and caps for it, a battered slicker for bad weather, and whatever else he could scrounge. Poor doings. His saddle was at the livery barn. He got everything he needed, including a sack of parched corn.

He threw the worn saddle over the strawberry roan, loaded up, and rode into the dying day. His first stop was the weed-choked boneyard, which was deserted now. The grave diggers had filled the hole and raw yellow clay mounded over Olivia, hiding death.

He got down and knelt beside that heaped earth.

"Not much with words, Olivia. I'm going to miss you every second of every day of my life. You came into it and made me happy. I was lucky. Now you'll sleep and soon I'll sleep, beside you, for whatever that's worth. Now I've got some business."

He started to rise, but the unsaid still lingered in him; the hard part.

"Olivia, I love you," he said, glad to let it out.

He stood a moment, feeling the bond between his soul and that which lay beyond. He walked to the edge of the cemetery, where a ponderosa pine struggled to live, broke off a branch, and laid it over the clay.

Then he mounted the roan and drifted silently away from town, unnoticed, his departure known only to the retired lawman keeping the peace in Blankenship. He rode through the town, a solitary graying man in a rumpled black suit, string tie, and boiled white shirt. At the last he had pinned his badge onto the suit coat. It seemed fitting. He wanted Castle to see that badge. Clothes tell a story. A man in a black suit wearing a silver badge would tell a story. He would, by God, ride after Castle wearing his funeral suit.

He truly did not know where to go.

Somewhere a killer was stalking his family in order to inflict more grief on him. And, ultimately, that killer was stalking him. What next?

Then he knew where to start: the great coulee. He rode out the rutted trace leading to Centerville, which circled around the southern foothills of the mountains. That's where he had encountered Castle; that's where he'd go to find him.

Blue crawled with doubts. He was abandoning his family. Not even Carl Barlow was in Blankenship. The old cottage was vulnerable. And yet he could not help it. And Absalom was armed, for whatever good that would do. Strange young man; his purposes private and cloaked from Blue, his bitterness manifest.

Blue encountered no one on that lonely road. He made his solitary way through the late afternoon, riding in silence, alert but drawn deep into himself.

He reached the great coulee that led from that road deep into the foothills, and then into Jack Castle's mountain aerie.

Chapter 22

For two days Blue rode that giant coulee into the high country. It formed a great slash in the land, as if the bedrock had pulled apart some unfathomable time in the past. What began as a channel in prairie soon changed to cottonwood-dotted parks, juniper, deciduous forest, and finally a canyon crowded with spruce.

He looked for horses. Castle must have stashed his stolen horses in various convenient spots, strategic hideaways where he could trade jaded mounts for fresh. Blue thought that would be a start: Quietly pull Castle's transportation out from under him. That might not be as satisfying as a confrontation with the elusive killer, but it would have its effect.

As he rode, he checked the branches, especially those that could be sealed with brush, and in time was rewarded. In one spring-fed box canyon naturally hemmed by limestone,

Blue found what he was looking for: Two of Steve Cooper's horses—the two stolen from Blue—were cropping meadow grass.

Good.

Blue paused in deep shadow in an aspen grove and waited. He marked the lazy passage of crows, watched a marmot sun himself on a yellow rock, discovered a cow elk cropping grass at the upper end of the enclosure. He studied the rimrock above, looking for a telltale glint or a color not quite natural. Nothing.

He noted that some red willow brush had been casually heaped across a narrow neck, pinning the horses in. Blue tied his strawberry roan deep in the aspens and edged through sunny open turf to the barrier, and found it was actually two strands of newfangled barbed wire stretched between trees and concealed by red willow brush. He found no gate, but the wire could be easily untwisted at either end.

He dropped the two wires and edged onto the meadow, keeping a sharp eye on the rocky heights above. The horses stopped grazing and watched him. He thought about keeping one, but he liked the green-broke roan better. He circled behind, and then gently drove them out of the branch canyon and started them trotting downslope. They would drift downhill. Maybe in two or three days they would arrive at the road.

Then he twisted the barbed wire back in

place, just to keep Castle guessing, and continued up the chasm that sliced into the high country. He wasn't quite sure where he was but eventually he would see some peaks, and maybe then he would orient himself.

He doubted that Castle would keep that plodder Blue had bought from the Centerville hostler, so maybe Castle was down to his original horse and the stranger's bay. It was a start.

That evening he reached an alpine lake at the foot of a cirque, a hidden turquoise jewel fed by a glacier far above. He found a mossy glen beside the waters, and settled there for the night. He had the lightest of outfits; his bedroll was a single blanket and his slicker. He had a hatchet, a bowie knife, a small tin skillet, a roll of thong, some lucifers in a watertight tin, some fish hooks and line, some parched corn. That was all he could carry behind his cantle. That afternoon he had dismounted at a strawberry patch and collected a quart of the tiny, sweet berries. Later he plucked up a dozen wild onions.

He eyed the boiling clouds hanging on the peaks and knew it would probably rain, maybe even hail or snow. At that altitude, anything was possible, any time of the year. He hiked the perimeter of the lake, stumbling over mossy deadfall, until he reached the foot of the cirque and found the rocky overhang he was looking for. He moved his horse over there, though it would have less to eat, and settled in under that overhang. He fashioned a fishing pole from an aspen branch and flipped a fly onto the dark waters.

The dry earth under the overhang showed animal tracks, too blurred to identify. He found deadfall everywhere, and stacked a generous supply within his shelter, and then added tinder. He moved the roan to another patch of grass and picketed it. Then he fished, working around the mysterious waters as the sky darkened and the sun failed. No fish rose. It was as if all of nature was waiting for the mayhem that would soon explode over this mountain paradise.

When it got too dark to fish, he stumbled back to his overhang and started a tiny fire well under the ledge. The kindling was damp and the fire offered no heat, so Blue sat back against the inner wall and waited. An occasional freshet stirred the air, and he knew that before this high-country night was over he would see nature's violence. He was lucky. Many was the time that he had wrapped himself in a slicker with no shelter at all, and was half frozen by dawn. Once he had suffered through three days of brutal cold and snow, with no shelter anywhere nearby.

He boiled the parched corn in the little skillet, and while it cooked he whittled a spatula to serve as a spoon. Nothing but mush to eat, but he would add some wild onions, and enjoy the sweet and tart wild strawberries, and be content. A man needed very little to sustain him. Olivia's love had always sufficed.

He moved the horse to another patch, and then downed his meal quickly, scrubbed the skillet, and settled against the back wall in peace. This place, and others like it in these silent mountains, wrought that in him.

What was it that Jack Castle had said a few days ago at the foot of the coulee? Maybe there was a clue in it. A hint of what the killer planned next.

A violent flash and a crack announced the storm. Blue had been in these on mountaintops, seen lighting arc below him, seen wet gales pound the naked slopes. The air, so still moments before, came alive, whipping moisture under the overhang. Blue unrolled his blanket and donned his slicker. He wished he had cut some brush to stay the whipping rain, but it was too late for that.

He did plunge out into the flashing darkness, found his roan, and tugged the quivering animal into shelter. No sooner had he reached the safe dark than the heavens opened, sheeting water that fell so loudly he couldn't hear anything else or even think. He wrapped his blanket around himself and the slicker over that, and settled against the rock, knowing he would sleep little that howling night.

The storm rolled out of the peaks, lightning

chattering and flickering and blinding, the cracks forming a continuous ear-splitting roar that echoed from one granitic wall to another. The smell of ozone laced the air. Blue huddled deeper, wiped mist off his face, watched balls of light roll down slopes and alight on the tips of pine trees. The very earth quaked. His strawberry roan whinnied.

For some unfathomable reason, Blue felt a need. He rose, withdrew his shotgun from the saddle sheath, and settled back with a barrel loaded with buckshot across his lap. That felt better.

Something was tugging at his mind, pressing and pushing to burst into his awareness. The storm stopped all thought. He huddled within his slicker, knowing only awareness, the train of his thoughts silent.

Then, suddenly, it was over. The great blasts swept to other corners of the mountains. The distant lightning flashed upward, reflected off the black lake. The roar of tumbling water lessened.

Tammy and Absalom would be back at her ranch. Blue's cottage, with its lilacs and roses, would stand empty now, and the weeds would start in the gardens that Olivia kept going just by touch. Absalom would be engaged in his business, the mysterious thing that had brought him to the territory.

The boy never had a chance to see his

mother. And Olivia never had the chance to see Absalom. The boy had come back on some kind of business, outfitted in the best gear that money could buy, just when Castle was released. Maybe it was simply to look after Tammy. The boy had always been protective of his sister. After all, what did Steve Cooper know about guns? He didn't even own a side arm. That had to be it; an older brother looking out for his sister. Blue wondered if Absalom had a sweetheart in Denver. There had been a few, but his son had not married. All Blue knew was what Tammy told him from time to time. She and her brother had stayed in touch.

Way back when Jack Castle was sparking Tammy and welcome in the Smith home, Absalom hovered around the pair of them, keeping a sharp eye out, as if he knew something about Jack Castle's designs and meant to thwart them.

Maybe it had been a good thing. Jack Castle had been pretty fast company for Tamara.

Blue remembered the sentencing, when Jack Castle was put away by Judge Byers for eleven years. That's when Castle, in manacles, turned to Blue and began a diatribe, his voice so low that hardly anyone five feet away heard a word. Blue was sitting in the first row of seats along with his whole family. And there was Castle saying, "Blue, when I get out, and I will get out, you'll see what I can do to you. You'll see what's in store for everyone in your family."

Castle lifted his manacled hands and pointed. "Her," he said, the finger straight at Tammy. "Him," he said, pointing at Absalom. "Her," he said, pointing at Olivia, who was not yet blind. "And you." Castle had cocked his trigger finger and pulled it slowly, then grinned wolfishly.

The bailiff stopped him then with a sharp rap and a shove, but Castle was not done. "You'll see! I'm counting the days, and then you'll see."

They had hauled off the prisoner, but all of Blue's family sat paralyzed. That moment had burned in the minds of his children, in Olivia's thoughts, and in his own mind all these years. They had all taken Jack Castle seriously, but that was long ago. There was that deadly quality in Castle's voice, a man committing himself at any price. But Blue had mostly put it behind him. Convicted men sometimes talked like that. Obviously, Absalom hadn't forgotten.

Now there was only Absalom between Tammy and anything Castle was intending to do, and Absalom offered no protection at all. Not against Jack.

Still, in some strange way, Blue was glad to see his long-lost son. Absalom had come home. He had come to help. Long before Blue was aware that Castle would get out of prison, Absalom was preparing for this time, making things more secure for Steve and Tamara and the children.

Maybe they would shake hands soon—a father and a son again.

Chapter 23

In the gray dawn, with thick mist hanging over the alpine lake, Blue threw off his blanket and stretched his stiff body. A perfect quiet lowered over that mountain basin. The uppermost peaks were starting to glow.

He studied the misty shores, the blurred escarpments, and concluded that he was alone. He led the horse away from the overhang and staked it on wet grass. He kindled a little cook fire, knowing the smoke would blend into the mist and vanish. It would be more parched corn for a meal, but corn had always energized him, and he would find berries.

Daylight now, and insight. He knew what he had been groping toward, and he was mad.

Damned Absalom, heading out here to look after his family just as soon as he knew Castle had been released. Damned boy, afraid that old Blue, worn by the years, would be no match for a killer sworn to kill the sheriff as soon as he got out of jail. Bought himself an outfit and left Denver within hours after he got the news from the warden.

It peeved Blue to think of it. Absalom would just get himself killed, and there would be another Smith family funeral. What did the boy know, anyway? He'd show that boy a thing or two.

Maybe that was the big secret; maybe it wasn't. Maybe Absalom and Tammy had thought their father was in danger; maybe it was something else. Whatever brought him here, that Denver city son of his wouldn't help any. Hell, now he had one more Smith to look after, and the softest of the lot. Well, he'd show his children a thing or two.

Blue fumed his way through a miserable meal, scoured the skillet with sand, rolled up his bed, tied everything down, and threw the saddle onto the strawberry roan.

He ascended a game trail that led over the ridge and into the next drainage. He would look for more horses, and, with luck, he might find Castle exchanging his animals. One thing about that posse; it might force Castle to move, and Blue intended to be in the path when Castle came by.

Blue rode cautiously up a steep grade that tested the roan's balance, topped a ridge, and stared down into a blank green forest that could hide anything. He edged the horse forward until it stood before a great slab of mossy rock that had fallen from above, and there, no longer skylined, he studied the vast panorama below him. A moving man sometimes wrought changes in nature, such as an explosion of birds. But the anonymous green conifer forest stretched silently for as far as he could see and vanished into blue haze far to the west. Blue could see from here to tomorrow.

A park in a forest like that would make a fine hideout; grass for horses hidden behind dozens of miles of impenetrable forest, whose game trails were known only to Castle. Yes, it would do for an outlaw. Blue studied the sweeping plateau looking for the slight break, the growth of an aspen grove, the hint of grass and sunlight that would reveal a park, and was rewarded at last. On a flat maybe seven or eight miles distant, he saw the slight alteration of green he was looking for. He took his bearings. Once inside that hooded forest, working around deadfall, with no landmarks in sight, he would have little to go on and could easily veer miles away from the park.

Still, there were southward drainages running through that vast plateau, easily traced with the eye, and the hidden park that attracted his eye lay on the third of them. That was all. Once he rode into that forest, he would have only one thing to go on: It drained to the south.

Blue loved meadowland and hated forest, where few animals lived and passage was choked. But that park would be the sort of hole where Castle would hide, feeling safe because nothing could ever penetrate it. And that's where Jack Castle was mistaken.

The sheriff touched heel to his strawberry roan, and the horse worked gently down a grassy grade and into the cold and shadowy forest, rich with firs and spruce and lodgepole pines. Almost at once he was lost in a world without sunlight, without direction, without relief. Its canopy hid the sky. He could not ride a straight line, not with downed timber and thickets blocking his way. A man could get lost and starve to death in a place like this.

But Blue knew a thing or two, and what he knew was that all game trails led somewhere—to water, to openings, to grass. And that was all he needed. He worked the green-broke horse gently around mossy trunks, through spindly lodgepoles, and then he did strike a notable game trail that showed signs of use. He found the cloven hooves of both deer and elk upon it, and blurred padded prints he couldn't identify. It was cutting across the drainages, which was more or less the direction he hoped to go.

He hit a place where limbs blocked passage, dismounted, and led the roan through the tangle, fighting whipping branches that threatened to scrape the saddle off the horse. Now he was in a featureless world. He could scarcely see blue sky, much less the mountains. He did not know how to walk silently. Every step cracked dry debris, so he snapped and clattered through the forest, not knowing whether he was going straight or in a circle.

He struck a mysterious gray rock escarpment carved by an ancient watercourse, and found no way up it. Even the game trail vanished. He was lost, had no idea what direction he headed, could find no way to get his bearings, and began at last to wonder. He could not even find his way back.

He studied the old watercourse with its walls of schist, and decided that it, too, ran south, draining the south-tilted plateau. He would have to abandon his westward penetration and follow the drainage south, hoping for a place to turn west again.

The horse didn't like it and peered wild-eyed at the branches, expecting to see a big cat in the limbs. Blue didn't like it either, but a man could go ahead or not, and he would go ahead. He could ride in that old watercourse, so he mounted the quivering roan and worked south. He needed to keep a sharp eye on the sun and find a place to camp before dusk, because once blackness hit a woods like this, he could do nothing but halt in his tracks and wait until dawn.

The drainage turned out to be another game

trail, so he followed it for the better part of a mile before he came to an opening to the west, and then he urged the roan up a steep bank of crumbling rock and found himself in a winding park hemmed by dense stands of lodgepole. Fire had cut this swath long ago. It was time to be careful. He halted the horse in the shadow of a noble blue spruce and waited. He could see mountains poking through the crown of the forest here and there.

It was time for some serious tracking, so he dismounted and began a quiet, systematic search for hoofprints. Nothing came to eye, but that didn't mean much. The grasses were so thick and springy that he could walk right over a well-used horse trail without seeing it. But he found nothing.

He studied the wandering west-trending park ahead, chose to stick to its northern edge where the shade was deepest, and then headed slowly into the heart of the great forest. He knew roughly where he was, for the moment. But passage would be hard because this entire plateau was knifed with schist ridges eight or ten or fifteen feet high that were invisible to him when he studied the terrain from above. Each was a barrier.

Night caught him two or three miles farther in, and he settled on a site where a spring bubbled out of a fissure of schist and into a weed-choked pool. He would no doubt fight mosquitoes, but he had no choice. There would be no fire; not here, not within a dozen miles of that secluded pasture in the heart of the anonymous forest. Drifting smoke told tales.

There wouldn't be much to eat. He could not boil the parched corn. He found no berries in this impenetrable evergreen forest. But Blue Smith was not born to complain, and in any case, if he soaked some parched corn in water for a few hours, he could soften it enough to get some into his belly.

No sooner did he get the roan picketed than mosquitoes whined in, a cloud of them surrounding him and plunging at every inch of exposed flesh. Blackflies found him too, whirling toward his neck and hands. They fell upon the horse, which lashed them with its tail and snapped at its flanks and withers. This would be a hell of a night.

Blue headed for the spring, found soft mud, and plastered his neck and face with it, and then his arms. He loaded his skillet with it and plastered his horse's face, and returned for more mud. By dusk he had coated much of his horse and himself against the relentless horde. But no defense could stop that onslaught, and he slapped at the mosquitoes as he wrapped his blanket around him and then encased it with his slicker.

He hunkered against a mighty pine and waited for dawn, which would come only after an endless night. He thought of Olivia lying cold, a blind woman murdered by a man without scruple. He thought of Steve Cooper, murdered. He thought of Tammy and Absalom, and worried about them.

The mosquitoes quit their whining sometime after full dark, and he could relax a little and enjoy the half-moon shedding yellow light on the little park. He heard an owl, and the answer of another. And he swore he could smell smoke, but that was his imagination working too hard.

Jack Castle was not far away.

Chapter 24

All the next day Blue pierced deeper into that vast forest, scarcely knowing where he was headed. Then, late in the afternoon, he encountered a hummock, dark with firs rising abruptly toward the top. He tied the strawberry roan and clambered up the steep gray talus-strewn slopes until he reached the summit, and discovered that he was standing just above the crown of the forest and had a panoramic view of the surrounding country.

The park he was looking for was scarcely a mile away, due north, fifty or seventy acres of lush meadow embraced by walls of evergreen trees. He had drifted too far south. He studied the country for a while, looking for smoke, for the disorder of birds, but he could see nothing amiss. Maybe it had all been a wild goose chase.

He memorized the terrain at every point on the compass from that aerie, a sea of green treetops stretching for fifty miles in some directions. There were game trails leading up here; animals used the rocky knoll. And men. There, on a trail leading north from the hummock, were the prints of shod hoofs heading in both directions. Someone had recently been using this very place. It was possible to ride a horse right up to the rocky crest, look around, and ride down.

I'm coming, Castle, he thought.

He settled on the rock and waited awhile more. Patient observation often netted him information, sometimes crucial information. But he saw nothing more. He chose a route downward over rock debris that would show no boot prints, and eased around to his horse, which stood with ears alert, staring at him.

He found some of his own prints in the soft needle-strewn soil near the horse and brushed them away. He led the horse to harder ground and then brushed away its prints with a branch. His concealment efforts would not escape close observation, but maybe Castle was getting careless. His sort usually did, especially in a sanctuary like this, insulated by miles of dense forest in any direction.

Blue mounted the roan and followed the parade of hoofprints north, the shotgun cradled across his lap. He paused frequently simply to listen, to catch changes in the rhythms of nature, to examine the shadows where danger might lurk. It took him an hour to negotiate the mile, but then he abruptly found himself on the periphery of the hidden park, amazed by a sea of thick grass watered by a runnel off the distant mountains. The copper-colored bay grazed nearby. Blue halted, slid off his horse, led it to the deep shade of blue spruce, and waited. He didn't mind the wait. He had learned to enjoy the natural world and to read it. He did not know where Castle sheltered, if indeed he sheltered at all. But there would probably be a camping place with a cook fire arrangement back in the trees that would dissipate smoke.

Blue decided not to penetrate the grassland but to stick to the periphery, deep in forest, even though passage would be noisier. He worked slowly northeast, staying fifty yards in, taking his time, working along a game trail. His patience saved his life.

An obscure black cord had been strung across that trail, the trigger for a deadly trap powered by a bowed sapling that would have lanced into him with enough force to smash his bones. Blue stopped the gelding cold, shaken. Gently he backed the horse up, and then dismounted to study the trap. So Castle did not trust the forest to keep Blue out. If there was one of these, there would be more, each of a different type: deadfalls, pits, alarms.

Castle knew Blue was coming. Grudgingly, Blue acknowledged it.

Blue chose a different course. He led his gelding straight toward the meadow and out upon it. Suddenly he was in bright daylight, visible to anyone there. In the quiet, sunbaked park he mounted the strawberry roan and rode close to the edge of the forest. There would be fewer traps or pits or deadfalls in open meadow, and he was willing to announce his presence rather than deal with deadly snares.

Blue rode straight toward the bay, passing through fields of indigo larkspur that sweetened this devil's paradise. The bay stopped cropping and watched him. Blue rode close, seeing no saddle marks or sweat or sign of recent use. So Castle was out on his other horse, the black one Blue had seen only once, the one with wide hoofs. Blue thought maybe he would take the copper horse with him, but later, and only if nothing came of this.

Where would a man set up camp? Blue surveyed the periphery of the forest, seeing nothing. Water would tell him. He rode to the runnel that bisected the park and followed it upstream until he found himself in a savannah dotted with copses of aspen and willow.

And there, thirty yards from the creek, was the campsite, nestled under a long-leafed willow tree that would diffuse any smoke. Even here, Castle had been careful. His fire pit snugged into an amphitheater in one of those little ridges of schist that webbed the plateau, which would shield the flame even at night. Blue had to admire a man who took such care even when surrounded by a barrier in all directions. A stack of dry wood awaited use, some of it covered by an ancient canvas.

From there it was no problem finding where Castle slept, where he kept a horse picketed, how he lived. The killer scorned amenities, built no shelter against mountain storms, kept his presence to a minimum, lived with nature. He had subsisted largely on game, which he had strung up, butchered, and skinned at a certain limb. Blue found the bones of several mule deer and one elk nearby, cleaned white by predators. But not by bear; he doubted that bears would pierce this deep into thick forest.

All in all, Blue thought, Castle had picked a perfect locale. But where was he?

If Castle wasn't here, he was prowling. Blue was disappointed. He had pierced to the very lair, figured out Castle's ways, gone where no posse would go, read Castle's thoughts, and played a wily game, but Castle wasn't in his hideaway.

Blue decided to leave a few calling cards. He would trip as many snares and deadfalls and traps and alerts as he could, and then ride off with the stolen bay horse. Castle would return here on a jaded horse, and have no replacement. Castle might work down the great coulee and find his other two horses gone too. And that would be the beginning of the end for the outlaw.

But it wasn't the missing horse that would afflict Jack Castle; it was the discovery that old Blue was still his match, that old Blue had smoked him out, found a place unknown to the rest of the world, a place that would shrug off posses, and that from now on, *no place was safe.* Let the man digest that.

Blue spent the next hour springing traps, slicing trip cords, caving in pitfalls, and triggering the alarms, which consisted of noisy sliding rocks. It was a fine afternoon's work. He found Castle's spare tack hanging from a limb at camp, selected a halter and a lead rope, and easily haltered the bay.

Then, while he let his own horse graze, he boiled up some of Castle's cached beans, replenished his own food stocks, took every last bag and tin of grub from Castle's larder—rolled oats, corn, flour, beans, coffee, sugar, tins of tomatoes—and hauled them into a tight hollow right in the heart of the meadow, where they would lie unobserved even by Castle's keen senses.

Then Blue hunted down the most-used trail out of the park. That proved to be a game trail heading due north, much to Blue's surprise, and Blue followed it cautiously, his shotgun at the ready. The bay trotted along behind, offering no trouble.

But at a rocky spur the trail divided; one east, one west. The eastern one would probably arrive in Blankenship by some roundabout route, and the western one would head toward Centerville. Blue chose Centerville. If Castle was stalking, it would be around Tammy's ranch.

Blue headed down that game trail, which showed signs of heavy use, and was caught in deep forest at dusk. He knew he was going to be too late to find a good camp. Castle's trail was loaded with deadfall and low limbs, and would jail Blue the moment the light failed. It was going to be a tough night, at least until the moon rose. Blue tried hard to remember what time it had risen last night, but couldn't. He only knew that if he didn't find some hollow in the forest soon, he would spend a parched, chill, hungry, mosquito-plagued night, and the horses would get no drink and no grass.

A storm was building over the peaks. Flickers of lightning pierced the forest canopy. Sometimes these mountain storms rode off in some other direction. Others simply hung on the peaks. And some roared down the slopes to drench the lower country. Blue hoped he would be lucky, but this one was off to the west, and that spelled trouble.

He paused in the dusk, the silence broken only by the whine of mosquitoes, and pulled the saddle off the wet back of the roan. He blanketed the bay, threw his saddle over that one, and cinched it up. Then he swapped the halter and bridle and clambered aboard the big bay, the horse stolen from the stranger what seemed like an infinity ago.

"Go," Blue said, touching heels to the animal. His roan tugged at the halter rope a moment and then followed. The bay nickered, as if he had wanted to carry Blue all along, and Blue slackened the reins. Let the animal pick his way. Blue hoped the bay, which had traversed these trails, would take him somewhere, anywhere. Blue's only concern was the occasional low-lying limb, but he rode low, protected his face, and gave the bay its head.

A flash of ghostly lightning revealed a narrow woods trail ahead. Blue pushed onward into full dark, illumined only by blinding white flashes, his passage lost amid a continuous boom of distant thunder.

Then the bay burst into an opening, and just beyond into open country, as if a knife had cleaved the upland slopes from the forest. A chattering burst of lightning startled the horses, but even more did it startle Blue. Ahead, beside a rushing creek, stood a horseman.

Chapter 25

One flash, then darkness. Blue kicked the bay hard left, knowing a bullet would pierce the blackness where he had been an instant before. But none came. Blue waited for the next flash, his old Navy revolver in hand, and when it came—a stuttering of light—the horseman was gone.

Blue moved again, never staying in the same place, but zigging back to the right, waiting for the shots that didn't come. He kept moving, letting the nervous bay take him closer. The next jolt of lightning revealed no one.

No rain had fallen, and possibly none would because this mountain cloudburst was whipping away beyond the peaks. But the roar of distant thunder was almost constant.

It had to be Castle, and Blue itched to race into the slopes ahead, but he knew that meant either death at any ambush point, or loss of the trail, which could lead in any direction. He would have to wait until light, circle until he found tracks, and then follow the trail in the soft, moist soil. He was close now, closer than he had been for weeks. Castle was probably heading for his forest refuge when they met. The lightning was fading fast, and darkness engulfed this place.

Blue stilled all his instincts to give chase, headed for that brook, let his horses drink, and dismounted. His flesh crawled. Castle was fully capable of sneaking back on foot. Blue led his horses fifty yards down the creek until he found a thicket of red willow brush and pulled his animals into the screening foliage. At least no one could enter without crackling the deadfall underfoot.

Tomorrow, as soon as the light quickened, he would follow that fresh set of hoofprints, and, by God, nothing would stop him until he had Jack Castle dead or alive.

The horses were hungry and restless in the brush, but Blue couldn't let them graze—not yet. He pulled his slicker and blanket off the cantle, settled against a rough rock, and waited. Man-hunting was mostly waiting and pouncing, and now he was waiting in the pitch dark, the lightning a faint flicker beyond the sawtooth peaks. He heard the sounds of nightlife anew: a croaking frog, the scrape of crickets, the small squeaks of nocturnal roamers.

The half-moon topped an eastern ridge, swathing the high country in amber light. Wearily, Blue haltered his horses and slowly led them out of the brush and picketed them on the lush creek-side grass. Then he settled in deep shade under the low boughs of a sentinel pine and waited for dawn. He was hungry, but there would be no cooking this night.

He felt his heart toil heavily in his chest, and knew he had pushed himself to his limits. He hated like hell to admit that his body was slowly aging or that he could no longer do his job the way he did it in his prime. Everything ached. He needed sleep and couldn't sleep; he needed to stay awake and alert but couldn't do that either. Death, pursuit, bad food, days in the saddle—all had taken their toll, and not even a stubborn old man could cope with the betrayals of his flesh.

But stubbornness is what defined Blue. He ignored his weariness, hunkered deep into the roots of the tree, and thought about cutthroat trout, the warm bright moon, and the sweetest moments with Olivia through those fine years of living.

Dawn startled him, and he realized he had dozed a little. He studied the peaceful mountain country, wondering what lurked off in the haze. He buckled his belt and holster into place and walked quietly back to the place where he had seen that horseman, wondering if it had been an apparition. The tracks made it plain that it hadn't been.

He followed them for a few yards, a clear trail angling south and west, heading for lower country. He had a fresh trail, and one that would take him to the man he wanted. This time he would outrun Castle.

Awhile later, after he had downed some boiled oats and got the horses saddled and loaded, he started along that fresh trail, his shotgun lying coldly across his lap.

He rode all that morning, tracking along a trail that was so clear a greenhorn could have followed it. Castle obviously didn't much care whether Blue was following him or not. The hoofprints of a well-shod horse proceeded inexorably through meadow, over the brown needle floors of forests, straight across creeks, over rocky ridges, and finally into mixed evergreen and aspen forest at much lower altitude.

There in a quiet park Blue paused to stretch. He swung a leg over the tired roan and felt the earth jar his feet.

"Looking for me?"

The sharp voice scraped from behind. He swung around, crouching, bringing the shotgun with him, only to discover Absalom standing ten yards back, unarmed, hands at his side, his fine, stiff duds looking strange in this wild.

"You!"

"You've been following me since last night."

"You! Where's Castle?"

"Who knows?"

"Why are you here?"

"You going to quiet down and talk or not?"

"Not until I find out what the hell you're doing, leading a sheriff on some wild-goose chase."

"I didn't lead you anywhere. Following me was your decision."

"What are you doing here?"

"Looking after you."

"Looking after me! You're the one needs looking after."

Absalom didn't reply. His gaze was unblinking.

Blue was furious. "How'd you get behind me?"

"What you mean is, How did some tenderfoot like you outsmart me, the old sheriff. That's what you're saying. That's why I'm here. Because *I can get behind you.*"

Blue growled. He lumbered over to his son and faced him down. "I want answers. Now."

"I just told you."

"Told me?"

"You're not ready to listen yet. I guess I'll be going."

"The hell you will."

"You'll stop me? With what? That shotgun?"

"I damn well will."

Absalom started to walk off.

"Boy! Give me some answers."

Absalom stopped. "When you're ready."

"Do you realize that right now Jack Castle might have us lined up in his buck-horn gun sights?"

"You're not ready to listen to me."

"You're up in these mountains looking to get yourself killed, city boy like you."

Absalom headed for a shady dell and settled in the grass. Blue followed, full of questions.

"Where's your horse, boy?"

"Far enough away to keep him silent."

"How'd you know where to find me?"

"I didn't. But if I were Sheriff Blue Smith hunting the man who murdered his wife, I'd go where posses won't look. Like that forest. Hundreds of square miles of it. Pretty good hideout. You found Castle's hideaway, right? That park, the one you can see if you look hard and you have a sense of the land, that's it. I knew you were in there. I'm right, aren't I?"

Blue wasn't going to admit that his tenderfoot son was right about anything. "Where's Tammy?"

"At her ranch."

"Why aren't you guarding her?"

Absalom shrugged. "I'll tell you when you're ready to listen."

"I'll listen. Make it fast. I don't have time to waste on explanations."

Absalom laughed. The boy looked lanky and

strong, and life outdoors had darkened his flesh and given him a glow. But he still looked like a greener in all those fancy duds. Boy, hell, he was just about thirty.

"You tell me something," Blue said. "Long ago, when Jack was sparking Tammy, did anything happen?"

"What do you mean?"

"You know what I mean. Did he . . . outrage her?"

Absalom stared. "How would I know?"

"You telling me the truth?"

"No, he didn't. I'm pretty sure of it. He brags a lot. He couldn't have kept it quiet. And Tammy would have howled if he'd done anything. But why? Why that now?"

"You hiding something from me? What are you two up to?"

Absalom pulled into himself. "If you don't trust me to tell you the truth then you wouldn't believe anything I say. You obviously don't trust Tammy, either. Not back then, and not now."

Blue didn't retreat. "I'm making it my business. You hear me?"

"I shouldn't have stopped you," Absalom said. He stood, brushed debris from his pants, and walked away.

"Where the hell are you going?"

Absalom turned. "I'm over twenty-one. Where I'm going is my business."

Blue chewed furiously on that, even as his son hiked away, heading upslope and into some woodlands.

"Wait!"

But the son continued to show his back to his father.

Blue squinted at the hazy ridges, looking for the flash of metal, the stirring of birds, but the day remained peaceful. That boy had learned a few things after all, getting around behind him like that, making himself at home in the big country. Not very many men could get around Blue and come up behind.

The boy was trying to talk to him, to explain himself, but he was still so touchy he'd rather walk away than please his father. Blue knew the reason but hated like hell to admit it: When Castle got out, Tammy and Absalom figured old Blue Smith needed help, and knew Blue would never admit it. Blue snorted. He had a killer to catch, and now he would have to look after Absalom, too, because if Castle caught Absalom in his gun sight, there'd be another funeral.

What the hell was that boy doing?

Now Blue had a dead trail. He retreated to his strawberry roan and pulled himself up and into the saddle. Funny how it seemed harder every time he clambered onto a horse. He collected the halter rope for the bay, and pondered his next move.

But he didn't have one.

Chapter 26

Cold trail. But maybe that didn't matter so much. Blue didn't need a trail. Jack Castle would have his revenge—torment Blue all he could—and that's all Blue needed to go on.

The sheriff sat tautly on the strawberry roan, thinking that his son would be the next target. Absalom needed looking after, and Blue was going to protect that boy, no matter what it cost. That boy and Tammy were all he had, all he could call his future, all that he cared about, all that he loved. By God, he'd get Jack Castle before Castle harmed any more Smiths.

Quietly, Blue steered his horse in the direction that Absalom had walked away, and soon picked up faint boot prints here and there. Blue followed slowly, keeping a sharp eye on the ridges, taking his time. He would shadow the boy.

He wondered where the posse was: Maybe it

didn't matter. There were seven hundred square miles of territory to cover; the only good the posse might achieve would be to drive Castle toward Blue.

The sheriff found where his son had tied his horse. There were fresh green apples on the ground. Blackflies hovered around the pile. He kicked one apple open and studied its texture. His son's horse probably had good teeth and was young. Blue recognized some upland grasses in the manure; fescue, perhaps. The nearby hoofprints were elongated.

Soon he was on his son's trail once again, praying that he could reach Castle before the killer killed one more Smith. Absalom was drifting toward Centerville; probably toward Tammy's ranch. Plainly, the boy had taken Blue's advice after all and gone to safeguard his sister.

Blue paused in deep shade, studying the silent ridges, wishing he could see better than he did. Time had blurred his vision. He used spectacles when he read, but scorned such crutches out in the open country. But he was, by God, just as good as ever.

Blue knew a faster way: straight down that great coulee that formed an artery into the mountains. He cut over a ridge, and another, until he found himself in that long, green trough that had been Jack Castle's lonely railroad. Blue figured that if he hurried, he could put himself ahead of Absalom, which is where he wanted to be. Damned boy. Blue was chasing the most dangerous and blood-soaked killer he had ever dealt with, and there was Absalom, mucking around the mountains.

Blue rode hard for an hour and then reined his horses abruptly. There in the grass was a fresh pile of manure, still green, but beginning to brown in the hot sun. Blue shot glances at the slopes, studied the coulee, and decided to have a look. He dismounted from the roan, kept the halter rope of the bay in hand, and hunkered over this pile of horse manure. He pried it open with a stick. It was hard to tell, but he thought it had dropped from another horse. Its texture was coarser, the leaves broader; probably brome grass.

I'm coming, Castle.

He could find no prints nearby, but as he circled he did pick up a faint trail, mostly fresh-crushed grass, heading toward the west ridge of the coulee. He had to hunt hard to see where it led. The rider had artfully avoided bare earth, and his passage had been like a feather drifting across the land.

Blue pulled his shotgun from its sheath. Maybe this time Castle didn't know he was being followed. Maybe. But Blue never jumped to conclusions when he was man-hunting. And Castle was too wily not to watch his back trail.

Blue topped the ridge, kept low while he was

skylined, and then dropped into another drainage. The faint and sinister hoof marks preceded him. This was naked grass country, except for copses of trees that grew wherever they could reach water: willows, cottonwoods, poplars, chokecherry brush. Good bear country, and Blue reminded himself to be watchful. The faint trail led across a rill and climbed another slope, heading toward another ridge. Blue felt it now—felt the evil, felt Castle's presence. Sensed that nature itself recoiled as Castle passed by, as if the grasses had bent, the flowers had wilted, and the animals had fled in terror. Jack Castle, born wild, would be tamed by a bullet, because nothing else would tame a man without scruple or mercy or love.

Castle was cutting across giant drainages, vast creases in the land, as if heading toward a rendezvous with the devil somewhere. Blue tried to gauge the direction, which was south by southwest, and a chill caught him. The route would carry Castle straight to the Cooper ranch.

Blue no longer tried to conceal himself. He finally had an advantage over Castle. He had two horses, and Castle had only a jaded one. Blue could run him down. He pushed hard, avoiding any copses that might offer ambush, driving straight along the faint trail no matter who or what saw him, for speed was the answer now.

"I'm coming, Castle," he said to the wind.

No sooner had he said it than he heard the report of a distant shot. No bullet found him or even came close, but gunshots have a way of cautioning a man, and he studied the landscape sharply, aware that his sight was blurred. Castle had fired a warning shot, just to slow him. Blue halted long enough to switch horses, throwing the saddle over the bay and haltering the strawberry roan. If he needed some speed, he would have it with a fresh mount under him.

Then he was off, this time at a loose jog that ate up the miles but didn't weary the horse, and again he climbed a ridge and halted under its crest, his head barely visible to the horseman somewhere beyond. And this time he did see a horseman, maybe two miles away, a miniature figure caught in a vast land, and he knew it was Castle at last. And he knew Castle was in bigger trouble than he had ever been in before.

Blue rode easily, light on the bay. At the next ridge Blue discovered he had gained half a mile, but Castle was doggedly riding toward distant timber, crawling up a flank of the mountains. Castle knew he couldn't outrun Blue and was going to ground.

Blue rode artfully, his old skills taking over now. He was riding low and making himself small. He concentrated on the chase: how to keep Castle out of the timber. Plainly, the killer would reach that dense pine forest ahead of Blue and barricade himself in a hurry.

Blue was already projecting ways to beat Castle at his game, and the best was to veer upslope, hit the forest well above Castle, and then work down through the timber.

For an endless time, nothing changed. Castle spurred his jaded horse toward cover; Blue gained ground. Then, when Castle was scarcely half a mile from cover, he stopped suddenly. Blue mulled that in his mind. Castle's horse was giving out, and that's all that counted.

Blue veered slightly to gain the protection of a stand of aspen; he was coming into the range of Castle's rifle now and had to watch out. But his next glimpse of Castle puzzled Blue. The killer had turned his horse upslope and was not even aiming toward the timber that might have protected Blue.

What the hell was happening?

Then Blue saw Absalom riding down that slope, following a grassy drainage straight toward Castle.

"No!" Blue cried, but his voice wouldn't carry that far. Blue drew his revolver and fired it into the sky. Castle gave no heed; Absalom ignored his father, and rode straight at the killer.

Blue watched the distance close, yard by yard, foot by foot, and he could do nothing. Not from half a mile distant, with nothing but a shotgun.

That boy was taking on a rattler, a desperado who would stop at nothing. Blue spurred his bay and howled, putting the horse into an easy rocking chair lope that would let Blue drop the knotted reins, bring up his shotgun, and fire without being jarred.

Castle ignored Blue. He had his quarry in sight.

Absalom fired first. He stopped his horse, squeezed off a shot at Castle, missed, and jacked another cartridge into his lever-action rifle. Castle never slowed, but did make himself small, hunkering low over the saddle.

Blue's son steadied his rifle again and fired, and this time Blue saw Castle's horse shudder and stumble and begin to fall. But Castle sprang off with the adroit skill of a superb horseman, landed on the grass with his rifle still in hand, rolled over on his belly as Absalom thundered down on him, and fired upward at the boy.

Blue watched his son catapult out of the saddle, sail backward, and tumble to the ground, even as Jack Castle caught Absalom's mount, boarded it, and beelined for the forest and cover.

Blue felt as if a hammer had struck his chest. There was naught to do but watch Castle vanish into that timber a half mile distant.

The sheriff slowed, fighting his instinct to race toward his son. Castle lurked in those shadows not far off, and probably had his rifle in hand. It was a tough decision: risk a shot and get to Absalom, or wait and see. Blue decided to risk it. He spurred the copper horse toward his son, dragging the roan behind, and reached the boy without harm.

Absalom lay on his belly. Blood oozed from an exit wound near the small of his back. Blue leaped off just as a shot cracked from the forest. The bay shuddered, sighed, squealed, and toppled to the earth. Blue flattened himself in the grass. There were no more shots.

Blue wormed over to Absalom, turned him over, and found the boy alive and staring at him. His stiff new jeans and shirt were soaked in bright blood.

"I tried," Absalom said in a voice so low Blue could scarcely hear.

"Boy, boy . . ."

"You ready to listen?"

Blue nodded, pushing back tears.

"Tammy and me, we tried to protect you. You're getting old. You're too bullheaded to get help from anyone . . . especially me. So we had to do it without your knowing. Come here and stop him."

Blue started to protest, but swallowed back his words.

"We always knew Jack meant what he said . . . after the sentencing. That he'd get you, get us all.

"I kept in touch with the warden . . . he told me when Jack got out. Tammy and me, we made some plans. . . Not Steve. We kept him out of it. Help you whether you liked it or not. Even if you didn't want me to . . ."

Absalom was whispering now. Blue leaned close, straining to hear.

"Almost got him," the boy said. "Go save Tammy. She's next."

Absalom closed his eyes and died.

Chapter 27

Breath fled from Absalom. Blue peered into his son's quiet face and sobbed. He sat beside his son in the waving grasses, feeling the hot tears well from his eyes.

He cried for his son, for Olivia, for Steve Cooper, for the lives lost because he was sheriff and bound to uphold the law against the dark spirits. It was the first time in his life that he had cried. This bitter thing in him went beyond grief.

Bullheaded. He cried because he had failed Absalom, who didn't want to follow in his father's footsteps but tried when he had to. He wept because he had failed to save his son a bullet. He was too late, and he had been too late for many years.

A great quiet lay upon that sun-bright meadow. He reached out and clasped his son's tanned face between his big rough hands.

"I gave you life and took it away, and I hope your soul forgives me. I was a poor father."

A bright tan moth flitted by. Blue was aware of zephyrs stirring the grasses. He peered fearfully at that dark forest, its wall slicing the sunlit meadows from its shadows. Maybe Castle lurked there, waiting for his chance. Maybe Castle was waiting for Blue to absorb his son's murder before killing Blue. But no, Castle wasn't done.

The sheriff deliberately turned his back to the forest and stood. Nothing happened. The strawberry roan cropped grass. The copper bay lay dead, with Blue's saddle pinned under its side. Blue pitied the horse, another innocent victim of Castle's vendetta. So much horseflesh killed.

Blue peered about him at the innocent meadow, the shadowy forest, the rising snow-tipped peaks, the yellow blossoms of summer. Slowly, Blue unbuckled the cinch and tugged at the saddle. It didn't pull free. Blue twisted it from side to side, and gained a few inches. He was sweating now, using muscles that had atrophied long ago. When he did free the saddle, he staggered backward and fell, the saddle bruising him as he landed. But he soon had the strawberry roan saddled and bridled.

Then he slipped his big, gnarled hands under his son, lifted the young man, staggered under a weight too much to bear, and eased his boy over and across the saddle while the nervous horse twitched and sidestepped. Absalom's blood stained Blue's shirt and britches. With the saddle strings, Blue anchored his son across the saddle. There was naught to do but take his son away.

Blue stared fearfully at the dark woods, but Castle left him alone. So he led the roan down the long pastures, through the golden summer day, through lime green aspen forest, through ponderosa-dotted slopes, along a spring-fed rill, through a cottonwood grove where the silver leaves danced in the breeze, through the country his son loved to sketch—country he saw through eyes so different from Blue's. The sheriff thought that maybe Absalom's sight was truer than his own. Maybe it was the artists who should possess the best fishing holes in the untamed land.

Blue led the burdened horse down the slopes, out of the lonely high country toward settlements, scarcely knowing where this passage would take him. Centerville, maybe, since he was trending west.

Then, beside a laughing creek, he beheld an ancient burial scaffold. He paused beneath it, peering upward through cottonwood leaves to a platform of poles lashed between two gnarled limbs. He tied the horse, put one foot into a fork, hauled himself up to another fork, and looked over the edge of the scaffold. It was empty. Maybe that would be Absalom's grave, there amid the land he caught so well with his sure, quick hand.

Gently he untied the body of his son, lowered it to the ground, and wrapped it in his blanket, using saddle strings to knot it in place. Then he lifted it upward. It took all his strength. Absalom weighed more than Blue could ever carry.

But Blue would not surrender; not now, not with his only son, and by some force of sheer will he lifted the boy higher until he could roll him onto that scaffold. Blue's arms trembled. He pulled himself up the notches again and laid out his son, straightened his body, and lashed him to the platform. Then he paused, his heart thundering in his chest.

He pulled off his old hat.

"Son, I will grieve the rest of my days for you. I hope your spirit will forgive me. You loved the West in a way I didn't see. Your blind father failed you. And when I came into danger, you did not fail me. You came to protect me. You gave your life for me. Fathers should do that for sons, but you did that for your father."

Blue, his throat parched, swallowed hard. He rested in the crook of the cottonwood, spending his last moments with Absalom, flooded with grief and remorse. He reached out and touched his son's body, felt that lifeless form under the blanket, and then stepped down to the soft earth where the roan waited.

That was all the funeral, all the goodbye, he could muster.

He started downslope again, following the westering drainage to wherever it would take him, knowing that eventually he would arrive on the plains surrounding Centerville. He let the horse pick its way, for he had lost all will, and sat in his saddle without command or direction.

And so an afternoon passed, and as evening thickened Blue struck a two-rut wagon road—some ranch route—and followed it. Blue scarcely remarked the passage of the hours, for he was lost to the world. But in time, just as the sun fled, he struck the Centerville Road, and knew where he was. He clasped the horn of the saddle as if it were the horn of salvation, and let the roan go at its own pace. He had a long way to ride.

He rounded a shoulder of land and beheld a body of armed men walking their mounts his way, silhouetted by a rose-tinted sundown. They spread apart as if to confront him, but he saw Carl Barlow raise a hand, and the posse trotted up to him.

"Blue?"

The sheriff nodded. The deputy and his men from Blankenship crowded their horses close about.

"You all right?"

Blue didn't reply.

"Blue?"

"You catch him?" Blue asked, sharply.

"We combed a lot of territory, followed a lot of trails, but no . . ."

"Go on home, then."

Barlow pushed his hat back. "Blue, dammit, you look like hell."

Blue nodded. He didn't want to talk. Not yet. He didn't want their kindness. He didn't want them to know about Absalom. He just wanted to be alone and track down that outlaw because this was personal, so personal he was somehow relieved the posse hadn't found Jack Castle. Because if they had Blue probably would have pulled out his revolver and shot the prisoner dead.

"You got blood all over you, Blue."

"That's right."

His glare somehow silenced these men. "Give me a report, Carl."

Barlow slumped in his saddle. "We did a sweep. Half these men have field glasses, several more are good trackers. All we saw was tracks. Plenty of those. We never caught sight of a live man or horse in all that wilderness. We think he's fled the country. Did all the damage he could do and vamoosed."

"He was there."

"Whose tracks are all those, Blue?"

"Lot of horses up there, Carl. I'm on my third."

"You see anything?"

Blue nodded.

They crowded close, expecting Blue to relate his own story, but Blue just stared. They were all good men, volunteering their time and substance, and he should be treating them better, making them partners in all this, but all he could manage was a midnight stare that grew more and more black as the dusk caught it.

"Why don't you come with us, Blue?" Carl asked. "We're going to camp at Jasper Springs. You look done in."

"I'm on my way to Tammy's."

Carl Barlow saw how it would be. "All right, Blue."

"You done with us, Blue?" asked Gabe Leffwell, one of the posse men.

Blue nodded. "All done."

They stared uneasily at him. But Barlow, who was used to Blue's moods, motioned them on. Blue watched his posse, good men all, drift eastward toward the springs, and soon dusk swallowed them.

Now it was between Jack Castle and Blue; it had to be that way. It had been predestined from the moment that Castle whispered his threats against Blue and his family after being sentenced.

Blue steered the weary roan westward into the night. He was still ten miles or so from Centerville and wouldn't arrive for another three hours. Then he had another twenty out to

Tammy's place. Probably wake her up. Wake her up and tell her the bad news. Her husband, her mother, and now her brother. He wondered whether she could bear it. But she was tough, like he was.

Like me, he thought.

Blue thought of Castle, riding through those woods, thinking of ways to torment Blue still more. What was he up to? He had a fresh horse now—Absalom's gelding—and could move swiftly. But where? Toward Tammy? Uneasily, Blue considered it. Tammy was the girl Castle wanted and couldn't have. But that was long ago. Now she was the mother of two small children, and running her own place.

Blue suddenly felt a chill pass softly through him, and knew he should hurry. Not that Tammy was in danger; not with Cletus looking after her, as he was a swift, sure shadow who'd stop trouble before it came. Blue remembered how that hired man had put a cold steel muzzle into Blue's back before Blue even knew Cletus was there. Tammy knew how to shoot, kept herself armed, and wouldn't hesitate.

Still, Blue felt the need build in him, and pressed heels to the jaded roan. If Jack Castle was stalking Tammy, Blue wanted to be there. He knew exactly why he should hurry. Castle could have killed him up there in the meadow, shot him down as he stood over the body of his son. But he didn't.

Chapter 28

The clean, acrid smell of fresh hay filled Blue's nostrils. Sunlight awakened him. He peered about, remembered where he was, and sat up. The loft of the livery barn in Centerville leaked bright light through every knothole. He didn't know how long he had slept; only that deep in the night he had put his weary horse into a stall, hayed and watered it, and climbed to the loft without awakening the hostler, burrowed a hole in the hay, and fell into a stupor instantly.

It wasn't right that he should see sunlight, as Olivia and Absalom and Steve Cooper would never see it again. He sat up and stretched. He contemplated his blood-soaked shirt and britches, and decided he would get some ready-mades if his credit was good at the mercantile. He would let Zeke Dombrowski know he was in town, and then head out to Tammy's ranch. He didn't know how the hell he would tell Tammy about her brother.

The little monkey of a hostler wasn't anywhere around. Blue wrote out a chit and left it on the desk, collected his roan and tack, saddled up, and headed for Maisie's Place for some java, amazed that he had slept the entire morning away. He hadn't meant to; not with danger lurking.

Zeke wasn't there, but his cronies were, sipping coffee.

"Where's Zeke?" Blue asked.

"Some trouble south of town," one said.

Cold fear seeped through Blue.

"What trouble?"

"How should I know? Maisie said he got some coffee and rode out just after she opened at six."

The man was staring at Blue's blood-soaked clothing. "Ah, sheriff, you got something maybe I should tell Zeke?"

Blue grunted. He didn't want food. He wheeled out, boarded the roan, and headed south, putting the horse into a mile-eating lope. He pulled the shotgun from its sheath, kept a sharp eye out for ambush, and pushed the horse hard.

Worry clawed at him. It was probably nothing. There was no way Jack Castle could ride all the way from the high country to Tammy's ranch so fast. It was something else. But Blue couldn't put it aside, and it would be an eternity before he reached the place.

He scarcely noticed the howl of his empty belly or the lack of his usual cup of java. All he knew was that a fresh horse was too slow, and he wanted a railroad to carry him there at a breakneck mile a minute.

Not Tammy. Not his girl.

But even as he thought it, he knew Tammy had to be the next target; the final target before the muzzle was pointed at Blue himself. Castle's last stab at him.

Blue was oblivious of the beautiful and empty land as he thundered south. There was only Tammy on his mind, and the ghosts of his family rode his shoulders as he traveled. And Castle, the almost son and almost son-in-law who had murdered his family, the wild kid he almost loved.

The horse sweated in the July heat and foam collected on its withers, but it was a horse with heart and kept on going. Blue walked the roan now and then, but not long enough, and then put the horse into a lope again. The faithful roan was wearying, and Blue knew he must slow it down or destroy it.

Blue slowed the stumbling roan to a trot, and then a walk. He was still twelve miles from the ranch. If he killed a horse, he would never get there in good time.

Ahead of him waves of heat bent and shimmered the air. He felt the heat pierce his clothing, felt the sun hammer his weathered flesh, felt the grasses wither and brown under the blast of the sun. And then as he topped a hill, an apparition greeted him. It occupied the whole white sky before him. His family was marching up a long stairway into the heavens: Olivia, step by step, her face filled with light; Absalom, sharply etched, determined to master those endless steps; Steve Cooper, walking with great dignity; and Tammy, thin and proud, her skirts wrapped close, her chin high, stepping up those golden stairs and vanishing into the mist. At the last, she turned to look at him. He cried out, but she was gone.

The apparition was only that; the bleached blue of the hot heavens was all there was. Blue tugged the reins and sat the trembling horse, dismounted, and stood, letting the zephyrs dry him. Then he began walking before the valiant strawberry roan, leading it through the heat.

The wagon before him was not an apparition, and he knew everything about it long before his old eyes could make out the details. It was the Cooper ranch's spring wagon, and driving it was Zeke Dombrowski. Sitting on either side of him were Joey and Sarah, Blue's grandchildren. Blue stopped and waited. The horse hung its head, and its sweat collected on its withers and dripped to the parched earth.

Zeke stopped the wagon far from Blue, examined Blue, and then stepped down, leaving the little children on the hard seat.

"I'm sorry, Blue," Zeke said.

"Zeke . . ."

"She's gone. She and Cletus."

Blue couldn't stand. He slumped to the ground and sat there. Zeke hunkered on his heels beside him.

"How'd you know?"

"The son of a buck left a calling card. Tammy's hat, tied to my door. Found it first thing this morning."

"What did you find, Zeke?"

"Let it lie, Blue."

"No . . . I need to know."

"Let it be."

"I'll look."

"Blue, the children."

Blue staggered to his feet, walked toward the wagon, saw the two blanket-wrapped forms lying in the box, saw the pale and frightened faces peering up at him from the seat.

"Joey, Sarah, it's your grandpa."

Neither responded. He stepped forward and patted each one with his big paw. "It's your grandpa, and you've got to be strong now." He pointed to Zeke. "You go there with Zeke for a bit."

Silently they stepped down, landed on the parched earth, and walked toward the constable.

Blue untied the knots that bound Tammy's shroud and undid the blanket. She was white and naked. Blue recoiled. She had been shot once, through the heart. Her mouth formed a surprise. Her almond eyes stared straight at him.

Blue wrapped her again and tied the knots tightly.

Cletus had been shot in the back of the head.

Now you're coming for me, Blue thought.

Jack Castle was almost through. One last bullet and he would finish what he had sworn to do. Blue gripped the wagon, so dizzy he could barely stand. He did not know how he could let go of the wagon without tumbling to the ground.

The children had no mother and no father. He peered at them, ached for them. They were so young; almost too young to understand death, but not too young to learn that they would never see their mother again. They stared back at him from tear-streaked faces, as if he was the only thing in all the world they could trust.

He walked back to Zeke, who was holding each child by the hand.

"When you got there, what? Tell me the story."

Zeke aimed a worried look at the children. "Maybe eight or nine is when I got there. Tammy, in bed like that. Cletus sprawled on the porch. Got shot from behind as he came to see what the trouble was. Middle of the night, probably."

"The children?"

"Joey staring at his ma. Sarah still under covers in a trundle bed, whimpering. She heard it all."

"Joey crying?"

"No, just staring."

"That it?"

Zeke nodded.

"And Castle put Tammy's hat on your door?"

"Tied it to the knob tight so the wind don't get it." Zeke looked like he was about to crumple. "God, Blue . . ."

"They been fed?"

"No. I just bundled them up, got the dray horse harnessed, took care of things as good as I could. . . . You've lost Olivia, Tammy, and Steve."

"And my boy."

"No, no."

"Castle shot him, just when Absalom was trying to bail me out of trouble."

Zeke clutched Blue. "No, no, don't tell me that."

"It's so. I put him on an old burial scaffold. Brave boy, come out here after Castle was sprung loose, come out here to keep an eye on his stubborn old man. No finer boy, and I didn't know it until too late."

Zeke pulled his battered hat from his balding head and pressed it to his chest. "You've lost everyone, Blue. I don't have any words in me that do what words are supposed to do."

Blue nodded. "Mind if I drive this wagon?"

"Blue, you do whatever you have a mind to do."

"Mind riding shotgun?"

"I'd be proud to look after you."

Blue tied his tired roan behind the wagon and pulled off the saddle. Zeke untied his own horse from the back of the wagon and climbed on.

And so they started back to Centerville: the sheriff, the constable, and two small orphans. The heat bore down on them and rose off the clay to smite them and not even the crows were circling in the sky. There was only the steady clop of hooves and the rear end of the horse.

Blue's mind drifted back to those days when he liked Jack Castle because the boy would stop at nothing and that was the sort of man the West needed, and back to the days when he scorned his own son because his son wanted to draw pictures and be inside, and that disappointed Blue so much he could hardly talk to the boy.

But things didn't turn out the way he imagined. Jack Castle was the devil's own, and Absalom was the one with the great and good heart. Blue hadn't seen it; Blue hadn't seen a lot of things until now, when he sat in the center of the wagon seat, with two desperate little children swaying beside him.

Chapter 29

Blue sat in the parlor of Vinegar Will's funeral emporium, flanked by Joey and Sarah in their Sunday best. They were alone, surrounded only by dark space. The doors were barred to the clamorous public—half the population of the county seat—which had collected outside in ninety-five-degree heat.

Blue was damned if he would make a spectacle of this, even though Cyrus Meek, editor of the *Blankenship Weekly Crier*, was doing his best to sensationalize it. Blue felt uncomfortable in his stiff suit; he always did, but he would not wear anything else. Let the clothing fit the event, and this was an event most solemn.

Carl Barlow's wife, Millie, had dressed the children, and now they sat beside him, the threads of life connecting them to their grandfather. He reached out and patted Joey's shoulder and then ran a rough hand down Sarah's head.

There were no coffins here. Tamara had been swiftly buried in Centerville beside her husband, before the heat had a chance to work its evil. Zeke had sent an escort to guard the old sheriff and his grandchildren all the way to Blankenship, but word had spread, and even before they arrived at Blue's cottage a silent crowd had gathered. Blue was an object of horror and pity, and worse, a freak for P. T. Barnum's midway.

Vinegar was his usual officious self, and swiftly found a preacher for Blue.

"All right. Let him preach. But I'm bringing Joey, who's seven, and Sarah, who's five, and I want every word of it to be addressed to them, not to me," Blue said.

The preacher swirled out of the darkness. The parlor was curtained against the heat, and lit only by two banks of candles. Even so, the air oppressed Blue and he ached to be anywhere else than this close, dark, silent chamber.

But the preacher, a Mr. Fowler, proved up to his assignment.

"Well, now, little ones," he said, "we're going to say goodbye to your mother and your father, too, and I am going to tell you that they lived good lives. I will also tell you that most people are good, and we live in a garden given us by

God, and we must all find the courage to go on, in spite of loss and sadness and grief."

It was a good talk, and the children listened intently. Joey had suffered the most; he understood death better than Sarah, and he understood murder. He had drawn deep into himself, his gaze fearful, his tears hidden from Blue. Sarah had been stoic, but Blue thought the little girl expected her mother to return. Blue hoped the preacher wouldn't dwell overly much on a reunion someday in heaven; not for a five-year-old girl.

The Barlows and a lot of others didn't want Blue to bring the children. Funerals aren't for children, they said, and volunteered to care for the grandchildren while Blue attended the service. But Blue made his own decisions, and quietly insisted that things be done his way. It was an odd thing: The worse the tragedy, the more people meddled.

Well, they were going to receive some more surprises in a day or so, Blue thought grimly. And there would be more protests from all quarters. It was all well intended; people wanted to be kind. But no one ever quite understood Blue Smith.

There was something about all this:

Jack Castle had not killed the children, even though he had the opportunity.

The Reverend Mr. Fowler addressed the children kindly, and Blue was grateful. This man wasn't one to pretty up death, or even to paint fancy pictures of heaven and angels and harps and gold-paved streets. Often, the minister abandoned Vinegar's altar and stood right before the little ones and Blue, and there was a kindness in him that caught the spirits of Blue's grandchildren.

And then, after a prayer, it was over. Through a stretching silence, Blue sat in the darkness with his grandchildren. Vinegar fidgeted. Then Blue gently led the two children into the blinding sunlight and heat, where Blue's friends waited solemnly to receive him. Carl Barlow had done a good job outside, and he hustled Blue and his family to a carriage. Blue nodded gratefully and pressed Carl's hand.

The county supervisors stood there, hats in hand, and Blue knew full well what they were thinking: As soon as they decently could, they would ask him to resign. They would tell him what a tragedy he had suffered, how it was time for him to retire and spend the rest of his days fishing, after a long and noble career as a lawman. Blue nodded to them. Not yet. Not quite yet. Maybe later.

He surveyed the silent crowd, which gawked at him, at the bereft children.

"Come along now, Joey, Sarah," he said, and herded them toward the shining black carriage. Many hundreds of gazes followed them. Blue saw Cyrus Meek straining to overhear anything said and scribbling on a notepad.

"Clear the way now," Barlow said. "Make room."

Reluctantly, the crowd parted to let the carriage through. Blue stepped inside and sat on the burning leather seat. "Hot," he said. The children eased into place.

The enclosed black carriage swiftly carried them to their cottage, where more people waited, some with flowers or pies or pitchers of lemonade. They were most kind. Blue nodded his thanks from his carriage seat, and hustled the children into the hot, airless house.

Barlow appeared a few minutes later and set a guard around Blue's cottage. The grass had browned, and the flowers had withered under the blast of July heat, and the lavender lilacs of spring had surrendered to the sere tan of drought.

Barlow knocked.

Blue answered. Barlow stood there, straw hat in hand.

"You'll be guarded twenty-four-a-day. I've deputized half a dozen men," he said. "Blue, is there anything else I can do?"

"Fetch me a pair of mules tomorrow morning, Carl."

"Mules?"

"We're going up to the fishing hole and camp for a spell."

"The children?"

"What better place?"

"But Blue . . ."

That was as much as mild-mannered Carl would protest. But Blue knew a dozen objections were teeming in the deputy's head.

"Carl, you just run things here. Consider yourself the acting sheriff. In fact, I'll name you acting sheriff."

"But Blue, the children . . ."

"Two mules, Carl."

"Blue, that's where Castle started it."

"I know."

"I'll send a man along."

"No, Carl. Let me do this my way."

Carl Barlow stood on one foot and the other, sweating even under the cover of the porch. "I can't let you, Blue. You're just being bullheaded. Castle, he's young and quick."

"Yes, faster and meaner. Young, got good eyes, stops at nothing. Laughs when he shoots."

Carl swallowed, nodded, and waited.

"He'll find us there," Blue said. "Kill us all; the last chapter. That what you're saying?"

"Dammit, Blue, you're endangering the lives of those two in there! That's all that's left! All that the world knows it."

Blue stared. "Two pack animals at dawn, Carl."

"I won't."

"Suit yourself, then."

Barlow was on the brink of tears. Blue reached out and patted the man's shoulder. "I'm bullheaded," he said. "You're probably right."

"Dammit, Blue . . ."

"Good, fat cutthroat, cool meadow. Some mosquitoes, but that beats this heat."

Blue saw moisture build in Carl's weathered eye sockets, but then the deputy took Blue's hand and pumped it slowly. "It ain't over, but I got no say," he said. "I'd watch over you if I could. I'd watch over you till hell freezes over."

The next dawn Acting Sheriff Barlow appeared with two mules and an old saddle horse, too. "Put the little ones on that," he said, "long as you're hauling them to their doom, they may as well ride as walk."

Blue grunted.

"Dammit, Blue, you got three options up there. One is Castle kills you before those tykes, right in front of their eyes. Two is he kills all three of you, them poor little orphans, too. Third is you kill him right in front of them little ones, and they get to see a slaughter. What kind of sense is that? You'll scar them for life. Leastwise, if you're going to make bait of yourself, let me hide two, three men and myself there and we'll shoot that madman the moment he slips into that little valley, before he causes you more grief. The little ones, they won't even know the difference."

"Lots of fat cutthroats waiting for my hook," Blue said. "It's sort of a private place, Carl."

Barlow stared. "You're the most pigheaded man ever was put in office, and I hate the thought of attending your funeral because I'll be mad at you."

"Well, that's something for you to overcome, then."

Blue offered a hand, and Barlow shook it violently and stalked away. Light had barely seeped into the sky.

Blue quietly loaded his packhorses with plenty of comforts, including a wall tent with some mosquito curtains for the children and tins of corned beef. He didn't want to come all the way back to Blankenship because he had forgotten something. He stuffed his shotgun into the saddle sheath, wrapped his holster belt around his expanding middle, and pinned the badge to his shirt, poking it through the same old holes so as not to wreck the old shirt more. He usually didn't bother to wear the badge when he was fishing, but this time he rubbed the brass on his shirt to shine it up, and put it on over his heart.

He found a bag of horehound candy and some ginger snaps and added those to his kit. Olivia kept a few confections for company, and now Blue had company.

By seven he was ready. He hustled the silent children through some oatmeal gruel, cleaned up the kitchen, and hoisted Joey onto the back of that swaybacked old saddler, which turned to look at the load on its back and then yawned. The hush of morning still lay over Blankenship. Dew beaded the grass. The first woodsmoke of dawn perfumed the air.

"Guess we're going fishing now," he said.

Chapter 30

Sarah snuggled into Blue's generous lap as he steered the roan up the old trail. His big hand pressed her close and gave her what comfort a hand could give. Behind him, Joey rode the old swayback saddler, and the two pack mules trailed along at the rear.

Sarah's eyes were like Tammy's, dark and elliptical, and her frank, unblinking gaze was like her mother's, too. But now the girl lived behind eyelids squeezed tight, with the inner world safer than the real one. Joey was blonder, more like Steve Cooper had been, and seemed even more vulnerable than Sarah because he was at an age when he blotted up everything and ignored nothing. Blue could scarcely remember how it was to be so young.

They left the flatlands just as the July heat began to build and plunged into cool pine forest that breathed the fragrance of the eternal wilderness.

Sometimes Sarah squirmed, and Blue realized she was burrowing even deeper into his arms, as if she could not get enough of the thing she craved.

He listened to the clop of mule hoof on the clay, and the occasional snort and wheeze as his four-footed transport conveyed his small family into the wilds. He heard nothing else, nor was he paying close attention to the dangers that might lie ahead. This was a day for fishing.

The children knew he would care for them. That was a start. But there was a great hole in their lives now that he could not fill; only a mother could do that. He could give them Mother Nature as solace, but he was at a loss for words. In times past he might have told them that life is hard and to be strong. Now he couldn't think of a thing that would help.

Absalom would have known what to say, but when it came to comforting someone very small Blue felt as helpless with words as he would have felt wandering the streets of Denver surrounded by all those city sharpers.

They topped the forest divide, and soon he was peering down into the green meadows of his fishing hole.

"Pretty soon now," he said.

"Is that man coming?" Joey asked.

"I don't know."

"Are you gonna die?"

"I don't know that, either."

"Are we gonna die?"

"Not now; not until you're old and ready."

"How do you know?"

"I just do. What you need to watch out for is black bears. They like to pick berries this time of year, and they don't like people around. Sometimes they come to fish in my fishing hole."

"I don't want to see a bear," Sarah said.

He led his entourage down the long grade to the meadow, and then out upon the shivering grasses. He glanced swiftly at the place near his favorite perch were he had found the stranger's body. The grasses had grown there, and nothing remained to remind him of lost life.

The river ran, mysterious and swift, at the hole, pausing on its plunge down to the low country, harboring its secrets.

"We'll make a camp now," he said, easing Sarah off his lap and handing her down to the ground. Joey slid off his old horse.

"Here, Grandpa?" he said, pointing to an open but shaded hollow.

"That's a pretty good spot. It's shady and not hot. But I thought I'd teach you a few things," Blue said. "Now, is that a good place if it rains?"

Joey stared. "I guess not," he said. "It would get full of water."

"I reckon it would, son," Blue said.

Blue dismounted slowly, feeling his years in

his legs, and stretched. He tied the mules and horses to a picket line and surveyed the dark and mysterious fishing hole.

"There's fighters in there, Joey, big trout that will give you a tussle. I'll rig you a pole and a line after a bit."

He unloaded the packs and unsaddled the horses and put them out on grass.

"When can I go home?" Sarah asked.

"We'll make a little home here in a tent," Blue said.

"Will it have a mommy?"

"You'll be the mommy."

"Mommies go away."

"I guess they do, sometimes. But most don't go away. You'll be a fine mommy, and some day you'll have boys and girls of your own."

"If a man doesn't come," she said.

Blue dug into a pannier and pulled out the wall tent. He fashioned a ridgepole from a sapling and lashed it between two trees, and then cut tent stakes with his hatchet. An hour later, he ushered his charges into the tent.

"Here you are, now. There's more to do; ditch it so the water drains away."

"Will it keep the bad man out?" Sarah asked.

"It won't, but you will," he replied. "If you tell the bad man to leave you alone, he will."

It took a long time to set up a real camp. Usually Blue's fishing trips started before dawn and he ended up at Blankenship by dusk. But this time he was there to stay.

He hoisted the panniers with his foodstuffs high above ground, built a fire pit and lined it with rock, unrolled the bedding and let it air, sawed brown grass for the mattresses and spread it inside, and then reverently unpacked his fishing gear. His pole, which could be stored in segments and screwed together, resided in a tubular case, along with his reel. He had a canvas vest stuffed with flies, spare line, hooks, weights, and wire leaders.

He eyed the heavens; it was too early for fishing, so he cut a slim willow wand, trimmed it, and turned it into a fishing pole for Sarah. For Joey he manufactured a larger rod from an aspen branch, tied a line to it on one end and a bob and leader and fishhook to the business end.

"The man is coming, isn't he?" Sarah said.

"Maybe not for a while."

"He's coming." She rubbed her eyes.

"Sarah, Sarah . . ." he said. She covered her eyes and peered through the slits between her fingers. Why couldn't he think of what to say?

He assembled his own rod, hooked a brown fly and a small weight to the line, and then stepped to the place where he loved to peer down into the water, where the sun shafted deep into the crystal pool and sometimes he could see the dark forms gliding near the bottom.

This wasn't a good time to fish, and his shadow fell on the water anyway, but it might be a time to whip his line outward, to show two children what grace might exist in the swift, sweet cast, and to show them that their grandpa was not treading the earth in terror. He could live for the perfect cast, the gyrating line that settled the fly right where he wanted it to rest, where the quiet breezes of high summer cooled his flesh and swept calm into the children. He patrolled the bank of the hole until he found a low point, and then cast from the bank. He never fished standing in the water; he could not afford those English India rubber boots, which sprung leaks every ten minutes.

He gauged the wind, whipped his long line back and forth, arcing it farther and farther, and then let it sail out upon the pool and settle there. The fly touched the icy current, quivered in the embrace of the water, and drifted slowly downstream, untouched and unwanted by the cutthroats below. That was life.

Joey watched solemnly. Sarah had taken to the tent and curled up in her bed.

"It's the wrong time of day, Joey. The trout don't feed in the middle of the afternoon. They aren't hungry. They don't trust the shadows we cast on the water. Half the time they don't like the flies I hook to the line, either, and then I have to try something else. But I'm showing you how to do it. How to nail those big, fat fish just watching us from down there, their fish eyes never closing, their caution controlling everything they do."

"How come you aren't watching for the man?"

"Because I don't need to, Joey. Now pay attention."

Blue watched a fishing bird dive upstream. His eyes failed him and he could not tell what it was: an osprey, a hawk, or a kingfisher. He dreaded eyeglasses. He already had a pair to read with, but he was damned if he'd buy another pair just to look at birds.

The fly drifted toward the lower lip of the pool, just above the place where the river broke into rills and tumbled around gray boulders coated with orange scale.

That's when the cutthroat bit. Blue saw only a flickering around the fly, then a tiny pop and miniature waves radiating in a circle, but the fly vanished and the line spun downward. Surprised, Blue tugged sharply, set the hook, and let the trout have its run. The line rolled out of his reel, spun down the eyes of the rod, quivered tautly into the water, and plowed back and forth, left and right, up and down.

Blue was astonished. He hadn't expected to hook a fish in the middle of the day, while the sun glared down and he and Joey threw shadows onto that mysterious water.

This trout never broke water. It circled the bottom of that pool, headed for corners, reeled out the line, quit now and then, and let itself be drawn close before bolting. Blue let him run; a fish with that much muscle could snap the line.

"He's big," said Joey.

"I know. He's strong," Blue said.

"I don't want him to be caught."

Blue eyed the boy sharply. "Why?"

"Just because."

"Because we'll catch him for dinner?"

"Because he's trying to live."

Blue almost snapped an answer he would have regretted. Absalom had once expressed the same wish, that the fish deserved to live, and Blue had heckled the boy and called him a sissy. Maybe there was something to learn now. Maybe even a man of advanced years could learn something.

"He's putting up a good fight, Joey."

"Why do we have to eat him, then?"

"We don't. I'll catch fish for myself and Sarah, but you don't have to eat them . . . Lots of animals fish. Bears fish. They're very good at it. Did you know that?"

"Bears do?"

"Yes, fish are important in their diet. Birds fish, too. Eagles, hawks, kingfishers—they're all good fishers. Lots of waterfowl eat minnows.

And fish eat bugs and worms and lots of living things themselves."

"Yeah, they do," Joey said.

The cutthroat was tiring at last, and Blue slowly reeled him in. He could see the flash of silver now as the fish zigged and zagged through the dark waters.

"Do you want me to let him go, Joey? I promise I would."

The boy nodded.

Blue reeled in the fish and slid his net under it. It was a fine three-pounder.

"All right," he said, and set the net on the bank. The fish's gills heaved hard.

Blue clumsily undid the hook, which had embedded in the trout's jaw.

"Joey, pick him up now and slide him in."

Joey did. The trout lay on its side for a moment, and Blue thought it might die. But then it flipped its powerful tail lazily and sank into oblivion.

"He's a good fish," Joey said. "I will call him Silver."

"Silver he is," Blue said. "If we catch him again, I'll let him go."

Chapter 31

Some evenings the balsamic scents of the uplands drifted down on the breezes. Other nights the moist earth lifted its own pungence into the valley. Blue built cheerful campfires each evening to throw the darkness back from whence it came. When the wind wasn't blowing, smoke sometimes hung in the valley for hours.

He taught the children to fish, using nothing more than poles whittled from sticks with a hook and line attached to them. Joey crept to the river's edge where the water ran quiet and deep and cast his offering upon the dark water, and as often as not caught a trout. Sarah paid less attention, but even she caught a few fish, usually when Blue was guiding her, showing her how to whip her little line into a likely corner.

She needed her mother and was more fearful than Joey, who came to regard his life in the fishing camp as an adventure. But in the quiet moments, often when a lavender light settled upon their aerie, Blue could read the fear in their faces as night settled. He could not blame them.

Every other day one of Carl Barlow's volunteers rode in, sometimes with beef or tins of food, and always with news. Blue didn't mind. Let them look after him and the children. Each time a deputy rode down the trail and into the flat, the man peered about sharply, half expecting to find a slaughter.

But it didn't happen.

Something would; Blue knew that. But meanwhile there were things needing his care, and none more than nurturing the little ones in his charge. He had never done such a thing, and hardly knew anything about rearing a child, and now these matters were thrust upon him. His plan was to do as little rearing as possible. Days spent fishing and hiking and boiling up meals or frying food in a skillet or Dutch oven was an occupation in itself.

But Sarah, especially, had not forgotten. "Is the man coming now?" she asked each day.

"Sometime, probably," Blue said. He would not tell her otherwise. He would not betray her.

Then one day Jack Castle did arrive, riding casually across the meadow, down from the trail that vaulted up to that divide, riding Absalom's good stock horse, riding armed and confident, for the killer had long since ascertained with his spyglass that Blue wore no weapon at all, as he had set his holster and belt to rest within the tent.

So there was the man. Sarah squeaked a small warning and curled into a ball. Joey sat darkly, refusing to move. Blue stood slowly, set aside his rod and reel, and waited. In a moment he would know whether Jack Castle was beyond restraint like a rabid animal, or whether some shred of humanity remained in him.

Castle made a handsome sight, sitting the horse as if he were born there, owning the world around him, controlling all creatures great and small, as if even the sparrows heeded his every wish. But there was about him a knife-edged sharpness as he rode in, a gaze that swept everything and weighed everything, so that no sparrow avoided his attention.

The children found Blue's big hands and clung to them.

Castle rode close, his stare missing nothing. His gaze settled on a string of freshly caught trout that Blue was about to gut and fry.

"I'm in time for supper," Castle said.

Blue nodded.

"Of course, I don't quite measure up. The Smiths are too good for the likes of me. Aren't they?"

"You've answered your own question," Blue said.

"You going to invite me to light and sit? Sociable?"

"You will invite yourself, I'm sure."

"You're a good man with trout, Blue. Fry some for me. We'll have us a reunion. Just like old times."

Castle slid easily from Absalom's horse and stretched. "Nice horse," he said. "Replaces those you took. Evens it up, don't you think?"

Castle walked catlike around the camp, ending at the tent, where he plucked Blue's old Navy revolver, and at Blue's saddle, where he extracted Blue's battered shotgun. He smiled brightly. "Now it's more sociable, don't you think? Just between us old neighbors."

Blue felt the terror of the children as they clung to his hands.

"Come here, Jack," he said, standing up.

Castle weighed that, looking for a snare in it, and finally approached.

"I want you to meet Joey and Sarah Cooper, Tammy's children," he said. "Fine sprouts they are. Joey's a fine horseman and Sarah's got the sweetest smile in all the world. Just think, Jack; they might have been yours."

Castle's calm vanished. "But they weren't."

"That's right. And never will be. You had the chance."

"Start cooking, Blue."

But Blue didn't. "Joey, Sarah, this is Jack Castle. We have known him since he was a boy your age. We thought of him almost as a son, and many a time he had trout at our table, with his friends the Smiths."

Joey's lips trembled. Sarah blinked back her fear and clung all the more to Blue's hands. Gently, he settled her on the grass and looked to the cooking.

Blue built the fire and continued to fillet the trout with a sharp knife while Castle watched.

"It is good for little ones to learn civility," Blue said. "We'll welcome you to our table once again. And perhaps Joey here and Sarah will grow up with manners."

Castle laughed. Blue studied him briefly, and then returned to his labor. He set the blackened skillet next to the Dutch oven over the flame, which flickered inside a rock-lined fire pit.

"Blue, you're a card," Castle said.

"I'm old is what I am," Blue replied. "And that gives a man certain privileges, and makes some things easier."

"Harder, Blue, harder. You lose everything when you die."

"No, Jack. You don't lose a full life, well lived."

Blue stretched the filleted trout in the pan, crowding them close. They sizzled and spat fat. "If you'll watch over these and turn them, I'll see to the rest of it. Stir the potatoes. I'm not sure I have a plate for you, Jack, but you no doubt have some mess gear in that outfit of yours . . . that you seem to have inherited."

"Inherited," Castle said, amused. "Maybe I'll inherit me some more."

"Well, I was coming to that. Someone will need to look after these fine young people, and it may as well be you. They could have been yours. But you yourself made the choices. Here you are with another chance. Two fine children, bred strong and true, ready to be raised up to be a fine man and woman, long as the right father's doing the raising."

Blue's gaze met Castle's briefly. Blue returned to his cooking. He forked a potato and found it was still too hard, and moved the Dutch oven closer to the flame.

"Cut it out."

"I'm sorry to offend. I was thinking, here's your chance. Just the finest boy and girl a man could have. You could give them a home, comfort them, see that the twig is not bent, keep them in shoes and clothing and coats, put them through school, give them a trade, find a good husband for Sarah, set young Joey here with an inheritance of strength and courage, teach them your outdoor skills, teach them how to live in nature the way you do, show them what it is to be a man. . . . Are you up to it, Jack?"

"That's all, Blue. No more talk."

Blue nodded, flipped the fillets and watched them sizzle in the skillet, and then returned to his tasks. He fed sticks of kindling to the fire, watched the sun slide behind the northwestern ridges, suddenly casting shadows upon the old fishing hole, and kept an eye on Castle.

"Sarah, Joey, you run down to the river now and wash up good. I don't want a speck of dirt on your hands," Blue said. He turned to Castle. "Wash up, too?"

"I said don't talk."

"Well, I might obey and I might not. It's bad manners not to offer you the hospitality of this table. This is my home, you know, this old hole. I'm more at home here than anywhere else. Now it's my only home, my last home too, I imagine. But you take those children, now; they'll need a good home, and you'll provide it, won't you?"

"What the hell do you think you're doing? What the hell is the matter with you?"

Blue lifted a finger to his lips. "Watch your tongue, Jack. Little ears are funnels, and you might teach them ways of speaking you'd regret. I'm some guilty of that myself."

"God damn you, Blue, what sort of game is this? Scaredy-cat game, trying to talk me out of it?"

"Me? No, just wondering if you're man enough to bring up the children right and proper, because if you aren't, you won't like yourself very much for what you'll have to do to them. . . . You up to it, Jack? You up to doing what any good father would do: raise 'em up right? Because if you aren't, you're wasting time. Are you up to the hard way, or you ready to do it easy, two pulls of the trigger?"

"Shut up. Shut your damned mouth."

Blue shrugged. The trout looked about done. The children were returning, fearfully, holding their wet hands in front of them.

"You know, Jack, there's a right way and a wrong way. You do it the right way, after we're asleep, so you don't frighten the little ones."

"Shut up or I'll shut you up."

Blue began scraping the fillets out of the pan and settling them on tin plates. He stabbed potatoes from the Dutch oven and added those. He had butter, and dished some of that over the potatoes and fillets, and added a little salt and pepper, too. Then he handed out his meal.

"Well, here we all are," Blue said. "Joey, did your mother ever teach you to say grace?"

Chapter 32

Castle ate fast and hard, and when he set aside his mess plate his face had darkened.

"How do you feel? That's what I came here for. How does it feel, Blue?"

"You know that."

"You tell me. I want to *hear it*. How does it feel—wife gone, children gone, you waiting right there, six feet away, waiting, waiting?"

"How do you feel, Jack?"

"Don't spar with me. Tell me how it feels. I want to hear it. Hear it from your lips, you son of a bitch. I want to see the yellow."

Blue ignored him. He gazed at the band of blue over the mountains, knowing night was not far off. "It's the future that counts, you see. Two fine grandchildren, Jack, right here, carrying on. I put much stock in them. They'll do fine after I'm gone. Their mother raised them up fine."

Castle glowered. "Maybe you're mistaken."

"No, I'm right, aren't I?"

Castle laughed. "Who's running this show? It's not you, you yellow son of a bitch."

Blue turned to Joey. "Time to rinse these plates and clean up. You too, Sarah. You take these plates and scrub them good. I don't want bears around here messing with fish bones and getting into our packs."

Sarah stared at Castle and rubbed her eyes. She hadn't eaten. Joey rose fearfully.

"You just get Jack Castle's plate there, Joey, and rub it up in the river."

It was all the boy could do to reach for the plate resting in the grass before Castle. The killer smirked. "Afraid of me, are you, kid?"

Joey leapt back. Blue reached across to pluck up the plate.

"Leave it alone. The kid'll do it," Castle snapped.

Joey glanced fearfully at Blue, who nodded, and then he edged forward and picked up the plate. Castle dashed it from the boy's hand.

Joey yelped.

"Try again, kid. Afraid of me?"

Joey couldn't manage it.

"What kind of coward are you, kid? Some Smith you are! Worse than Absalom. Get that damned plate."

Blue stood slowly, knowing the moment had come.

"Joey, you take Sarah to the tent. It's bedtime."

Joey was paralyzed. He glanced up at Blue and at Castle.

"I said get that damned plate, kid."

Blue pointed at the tent.

Joey slowly crept away, heeding Blue.

"I said get that plate, kid," Castle snapped, and the revolver materialized in his hand.

"Go to bed, son," Blue said gently.

Castle pulled the trigger. The revolver bucked, the shot violent in the hush of evening. The boy whimpered, untouched.

"You take Sarah and go to the tent," Blue said, "and you'll be all right."

The boy grabbed his sister and bolted.

"Damn you, Smith. Damn all of you."

Blue knew he had won. It was such a simple, offhand thing, trouble over nothing of consequence; a plate, a child, a command. But it was the crucial moment, the thing Blue had waited for.

Fearfully, Joey pulled Sarah with him toward the canvas tent, whose brown sides were no protection at all from Jack Castle, and yet would now be a fortress. The flap flew open and closed behind them.

Blue heard Sarah's sobs.

"You see?" Blue said.

"That doesn't mean a thing. You're a dead man."

"All right. Go ahead."

Castle tramped a circle, cursing, waving that revolver. Then swiftly he stepped toward Blue and jammed the revolver into Blue's gut.

"I took it all away, didn't I?"

"No, Jack. I've got some things you can't have. Even now."

"But not life."

"Honor."

"You took it all from me. I wasn't good enough. You packed me off and now I got nothing."

"A noose or a bullet, yes, and no honor."

Castle spasmed, and Blue wondered whether the trigger finger would spasm too.

"I made some mistakes," Blue said. "I've got that, too, the bad mistakes. Absalom . . ."

"Yeah, he was a mistake all right."

"No, Jack, he came out fine. The mistake was mine."

Castle yanked his revolver away, stepped back, and grinned. Blue could see the grin even in the creeping blackness.

"Make you dance," he said. "Dance like a pilgrim."

A shot shocked the night. Blue felt a bullet plough dirt at his feet. Another shot, violent on his ears, nicked his boot heel. Another seared through his pants. Blue didn't move.

Castle shot the hat off Blue's head, blew Blue's wicker creel into pieces, fired between

Blue's legs, and another shot seared Blue's hip. Then the revolver clicked.

Castle jammed it into his holster.

"Just you try me and see," he said.

"I'm not."

"You got me into this. You wrecked me. First you told me to be tough, be strong, don't take guff from anyone, don't be like Absalom. You didn't say that in words, but you said it. So I'm what you made me."

Blue nodded. There was a dark and sad truth in it.

"Then I was king of the world. There wasn't no one in Blankenship could do what I could do. And you didn't mind when I came visiting Tammy, neither."

Blue nodded.

"You hardly never said no to me; when I run a little fast what did you do? You just smiled, like I was the real son. And then what? Next thing I knew, I wasn't welcome. And you were warning Tammy off, so she gets upset around me. And you never told me why."

Blue felt Castle's accusations seep through him, stain him.

"So it's maybe your fault too, only now I got no place to go. You did that to me."

"No, you crossed the lines yourself, Jack."

"What are you doing, arguing with me? You shut up."

Blue nodded.

"You wrecked me, that's what. You showed me how to be tougher than anyone. Then I wasn't good enough for you. Jack Castle wasn't up to the Smiths. And that's when the trouble started."

Blue forced himself to say nothing. His own contribution to Jack Castle's ruin tormented him, but not entirely. Jack had always known the limits. Castle had made his own life.

"I have to take you in, Jack."

"For what? The noose?"

"More than likely."

"Well I'm not going."

"You'll be tracked down. Carl Barlow's a good man. He's not going to miss a thing. There's wires now connecting sheriffs and lawmen around the territory, dodgers printed up. You can run, but you'll come to the end sooner or later. May as well come with me, Jack."

"Why are you talking like that? Me, with the gun, and you standing there."

"I'm taking you in."

"The hell you are. You're crazy. I got one loaded gun left."

"You're under arrest, Jack. Drop that gun belt."

"Are you mad or something? I'm riding out of here, and where I'm going you'll never find me. You can search for me the rest of your life and never find me. You can ride a horse ten feet away and never know. You can find my horses and my gear and never see me again."

"Is that a deal?"

"What do you mean, a deal?"

"I stop coming for you . . . because I don't have to."

Castle stared into the fire, his eyes red coals.

"You put me down as missing. You hear me? Missing. Jack Castle was never caught. Jack Castle will still be wanted, ten years, fifty years, from now. You put me down as missing?"

"Missing," Blue said.

"Well, goodbye then. I don't know why I'm letting you off."

"I guess you had to, Jack."

"It's your fault. You got me started. Now you put me in a bind and there's no way out."

Blue sighed. There had always been ways out. Castle hadn't listened or heeded the lessons.

"Is it a deal?" Blue asked.

"Maybe."

"Yes or no. Otherwise I'm coming for you."

Castle's eyes glowed red in the coals of the fire. "How much time have I got?"

"None."

"I could just kill you. That's what I should have done. End this."

"Yes, you could."

"I'm taking two days. You hear me, Blue? You

don't come after me, not now, not ever, and in two days you won't need to."

"I'll fish."

"Fish!"

"We'll be right here, catching cutthroats and camping."

"Damn you, Blue, for messing me up."

"I'm not proud of anything I've done to mess you up."

Castle stared into the blackness. "All right. There's no way out, anyway. In two days you won't have a reason to come after me."

"Your word is your bond. That's one of the good things in you. There are other good things."

"Dammit, Blue, didn't you know? How much I wanted . . ." There were tears in Castle's voice. The darkness cloaked the rest of him.

Blue stood quietly while Jack Castle climbed aboard Absalom's horse and rode into the night. For a while he could hear the fall of the hoofs, and then he heard nothing.

Chapter 33

It was raining. Long before daylight, Blue lay in his bedroll listening to the patter of water on canvas. The tent leaked a little, and water slid down the underside of the old cloth and dripped onto a corner near Joey's feet.

It was plenty cold, and he wished he had more blankets to shield the children from the weather. He hadn't slept much. The children lay under their blankets, choked with fear, and Blue had spent much of the evening lying between them, his big arms drawing each child to his side.

He was a man of few words, and could say only one thing: The man was gone and would not come back.

Now it rained. In time, he discerned a subtle change in the light and knew another day was upon them. He threw off his blanket, opened the flap, and beheld a meadow wrapped in mist. The peaks had vanished behind white veils, the river ran black and somber, the trees had been darkened by wetness. A chill, moist breeze confronted him.

He closed the flap, preferring the gloom and tender warmth of the tent. Joey was staring at him. Blue smiled, clasped the boy's hand, and held it. Sarah, still exhausted by terror, lay in a ball, her thumb in her mouth.

The rain fit his mood. He didn't really want to waken to an idyllic and golden day at the fishing hole. He thought of Jack Castle, bone cold and wet, hopeless and futureless and doomed, somewhere in the mountains preparing for his fate. Things had to end that way. It was a far better ending than any other.

He wondered where Castle would go, how he would do what he had to do, and then Blue knew intuitively. It was so simple. The thought awakened a bitterness, but Blue set it aside. What would be would be.

He lay in his bedroll until he no longer could, and then he pulled the tent flap aside and slid outside, feeling the shock of icy water pelt him. He might be a weather-hardened man, but this numbing rain was no picnic. He performed his ablutions hastily, eyed his rain-soaked pile of kindling, and knew they would have no fire soon.

He studied the meadow, found the horses

lost in mist yonder, and returned to the tent, shivering. Now Sarah was awake too.

"Is the man coming?" she asked.

"The man is gone and will never come back."

"Not ever?"

"Not ever."

The answer didn't satisfy her, and she glanced fearfully at the flap.

"Let's catch us a good breakfast," Blue said.

He hurried the reluctant children through their morning chores and to the riverbank. The drizzle was letting up, and soon they scarcely noticed it. The trout were jumping. Even Sarah, who had not much enjoyed fishing, was caught up in the excitement as she pulled in silvery fish with her crude pole and line. Her hair was plastered to her head by rain, but she didn't care.

Then Joey pulled in a big, flopping trout, and paused suddenly as he netted it.

"Silver, Silver," he said, a sudden ache in his voice.

"How do you know?"

"I just do."

Blue examined the heaving fish. There on the jaw was a ragged place, torn by Joey's hook days earlier.

"You're right, Joey. It's Silver," Blue said.

Joey swiftly unhooked his brown fly and slid the fish back into the cold water. He was grinning.

"He let me catch him again."

"Sometimes a creature wants to be caught," Blue said, "and released."

Blue stared at the ridges, visible now through the white veils. The great slopes rose black into the skies, as grand as ever, but lonely now. He felt a deep sadness steal through him. He wondered how he could pity Jack Castle, who had inflicted such grief upon Blue and his whole family.

By noon a late-July sun had burned off the white gauze of fog, and Blue built a hot fire, finding dry kindling in an aspen grove where a less experienced person might have discovered none.

The children were famished, but none the worse for wear from their rain bath and empty stomachs. He would raise them to be strong and enduring and able to think beyond the comforts they craved.

He fed them well: biscuits raised in the Dutch oven, trout fillets sautéed in butter, some boiled beans with a little side pork for flavor. The grass dripped with dew. Puffy clouds moored themselves to the peaks. The horses stood steaming as the sun pummeled the wetness off their backs.

That afternoon Carl Barlow himself rode in, bringing provisions from town, checking up on the sheriff.

The deputy studied the fishing hole, and then stepped down.

"I guess you have no news," he said. "Not much in town, either. You all right?"

"Better than before," Blue said.

"I guess whatever you had in mind didn't take."

"Oh, it took, Carl, it took."

The deputy stared.

Blue had no mind to tell him anything, but he knew he had to. A lawman can't be hiding things from his trusted men.

"He came and went last night," Blue said.

Barlow was amazed. "You caught him and let him go?"

"No, he caught me and let me go."

"Blue . . ."

"He couldn't do it. I sort of knew he couldn't."

"What happened? What did you say?"

"I told him he would have to raise up the children to be good and strong."

Barlow lifted his battered felt hat from his head and squinted. "There's something going on here I ain't getting a handle on," he said. "Where's Castle now?"

Blue shrugged. He wanted just to leave it lie, but knew Barlow would keep on pumping him. "Carl, you'll never see Jack Castle again. You'll never get wind of him. It's over."

"How do you know that?"

"I know it."

"He left a trail, probably hoofprints inches

deep in the mud. We'll go after him. He's up there, carving a trail that a fool could follow."

Blue shook his head. "Carl, let it be."

"Let it be! Hell no, I'm not letting it be. This is crazy. He's the most wanted man in the territory. In the West. In the whole country, maybe. No man's hands are bloodier, no man's name is more feared and hated."

"You give me a couple of days, and I'll be able to tell you the case is over. I have to make a little trip is all."

"What am I supposed to tell folks in town? That you let Castle go? That murderer?"

"No, Castle caught *me* and let me go. And the children too. You tell 'em that, and tell 'em we're fishing, and everything is all right."

"I'm going to worm this story out of you, Blue. Either that or you'll tell it under oath at some hearing. Is Castle alive or dead?"

"I'll know in a day or two. Right now, he's a fugitive and missing just as he has been, wanted dead or alive just as he has been."

"Why aren't you getting up a posse and going after him?"

It had come down to this, then. "Carl, there's no need for a posse."

Barlow scraped moist earth with the toe of his boot. "This is between you and him, then. It always was. Has been since he was a boy, and you were almost a pa of his. Still is between you, even if he's . . . put your family in graves.

Well, I'll do this much: I'll hold off the folks in town. I'll keep the *Weekly Crier* in the dark—for now. But dammit, Blue . . ."

Blue clapped his deputy on the back. "That's a deal," he said. "We're fishing here tomorrow, and the next day we're heading out. So you don't need to send anyone up here to look after us."

Barlow grinned and shook his head. "I guess you've got your posse right here," he said, nodding toward the children sitting on the bank of the fishing hole.

"You speak truer words than you know, Carl."

Blue watched the deputy board his horse and ride off. Then, with a small wave, Barlow vanished into the forest. *Good man,* Blue thought. The deputy didn't know it, but he'd be sheriff soon. In a few days, maybe.

The thought shot pangs through Blue. He remembered Olivia dishing out apple pie to Carl over dinner. He remembered standing beside Carl, best man at Carl's wedding to Agnes, and remembered Carl's good-natured campaigns to get himself elected sheriff. And now Carl would have his wish.

Times had changed. Blue had new responsibilities. But he ached for the old days, the times he could slip up here all alone, just him and the fish, and the mule deer out on the meadows, and the eagles floating over, and the snow on the peaks even in August, and his wife's arms discovering him when he returned, and the joy of a man with a family doing well.

The fish quit biting in the bright afternoon sun, so Blue gathered the children into the tent for a nap. Fear had not abandoned them, nor was Blue himself unafraid.

They fished that evening, and the man didn't come, and they fished the next day, and the man didn't come. Joey and Sarah had grown restless, and Blue knew the time had come to leave the fishing hole, let it heal, let the deer and elk reclaim the meadows, let the kingfishers dive for minnows, and let the spirit of the dead stranger depart. Blue had felt its presence, felt that first dark murder all the while, still wounding his paradise. Now with the thing that had come to Jack Castle, the spirits might leave.

The morning of the third day Blue caught the packhorse and mules and his own strawberry roan, dismantled the tent, poured water over the breakfast fire, slid his fishing gear into its place, and then hoisted the children onto the swaybacked saddler.

"I'll be with you in a moment," he said.

He walked out into the meadow, feeling its sweetness, and then lifted his gaze to the everlasting mountains, feeling their shoulders guard him, and then into the mysterious hole where the waters ran dark. He saw a flash of silver there, down some unfathomable distance below the surface.

He boarded his horse and led his little caravan away, not over the pass to Blankenship but up the steep trail, over the ridge, and across vast drainages. The children enjoyed the ride; they were glad to be going somewhere. The lushness of summer lay upon the land, along with a vast silence. He camped that night in a broad canyon, and fed the children from the stores Carl Barlow had brought them.

The next day Blue descended the slopes of the mountains until late afternoon, when he could see the high plain spread before him. But closer at hand was the tree he had come to see, the tree that carried in its limbs the old Indian burial scaffold where Absalom lay. Even as Blue rode, he saw a great flock of carrion birds, red-headed black vultures, gathered at that tree, burdening every limb. He knew he must approach upwind, for the downwind stench would be unbearable. And he must go alone.

He steered the children in a great arc around that tree. They saw the flocking vultures but did not grasp the meaning of those dark flesh eaters. He left the children a hundred yards out, sitting on their horse, and rode ahead to the burial tree. The vultures did not yield, but flapped wings and threatened him as he neared the place.

He could not see what lay above so he dismounted, stirring the vultures, and then scared them away with shouts and waving arms. A score of them lumbered heavily into the sky. He tied a bandana over his nose, thinking it would do little good, and crawled up one notch and then another until he could see.

There were two bodies. Absalom, tightly bound from head to toe, and Jack Castle, whose face, neck, and shoulders had been pecked away until little remained but bone.

Blue didn't linger. He didn't even seek to find the instrument of death. He hastened to the stained earth and backed away. One beloved and brave son whom Blue had twisted and hurt. Another man who had murdered most of Blue's family.

Blue remembered clearly the many times he had hiked and camped and hunted with Jack Castle, taught the boy the skills of the wilds, encouraged the boy to grow in strength and courage.

Had he failed Jack Castle as he had failed his own Absalom?

He knew he hadn't. Blue had shown Jack Castle what made a man, but Jack Castle hadn't listened to half of it, and the fatherless youth ran wilder and wilder until he crossed the divide that led straight to this early grave. In that moment, Blue absolved himself. More than absolved himself: He knew that Jack Castle would have gone much wilder, a lot younger, and died a lot sooner, had it not been for Sheriff Blue Smith.

He rode back to the children.

"What did you do?" Joey asked.

"I visited your uncle's grave," Blue said. "That's where I put Absalom, wrapped up in the Indian way and given to the sun rather than the earth. He's been given to the sun, Joey."

"I liked him," Joey said.

"I loved him," Blue said, and, strangely, the images of both the young men on that scaffold came to mind.

He would resign. He would fish. And he would see to it that his grandchildren grew to be what they most wanted to be.

SIGNET

Joseph A. West

"I look forward to many years of entertainment from Joseph West."

—Loren D. Estleman

"Western fiction will never be the same." **—Richard S. Wheeler**

Silver Arrowhead

0-451-20569-3

When the bones of the world's first Tyrannosaurus Rex are discovered in Montana cattle country—and the paleontologist responsible for the find is murdered—it's up to San Francisco detective Chester Wong to find the killer.

Johnny Blue and the Hanging Judge

0-451-20328-3

In this new adventure, Blue and his sidekick find themselves on trial in the most infamous court in the West....

To order call: 1-800-788-6262

S473

JASON MANNING

Mountain Honor 0-451-20480-8

When trouble arises between the U.S. Army and the Cheyenne Nation, Gordon Hawkes agrees to play peace-maker-until he realizes that his Indian friends are being led to the slaughter...

Mountain Renegade 0-451-20583-9

As the aggression in hostile Cheyenne country escalates, Gordon Hawkes must choose his side once and for all-and fight for the one thing he has left...his family.

The Long Hunters 0-451-20723-8

1814: When Andrew Jackson and the U.S. army launch a brutal campaign against the Creek Indians, Lt. Timothy Barlow is forced to chose between his country and his conscience.

To Order Call: 1-800-788-6262

S575